GRIMSTONE'S GHOST

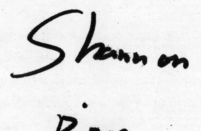

Shannon
Riggs

GRIMSTONE'S GHOST

MARY ARRIGAN

An imprint of HarperCollinsPublishers

For Emmett, Conor and Caoimhe

First published in hardback in Great Britain by Collins 2000
First published in paperback in Great Britain by Collins in 2001
Collins is an imprint of HarperCollins*Publishers* Ltd
77 – 85 Fulham Palace Road, Hammersmith, London W6 8JB

1 3 5 7 9 8 6 4 2

ISBN 0 00 675480 5

The HarperCollins website address is www.**fire**and**water**.com

Text copyright © Mary Arrigan 2000

The author and illustrator assert the moral right to
be identified as author and illustrator of the work.

Printed and bound in Great Britain by
Omnia Books Limited, Glasgow

CHAPTER ONE

I knew Mum was nervous. Her knuckles were white as she gripped the steering wheel and tried to peer through the rain-washed windscreen.

'I can't see a thing,' she muttered. 'Those wipers are about as useful as... as a colander in a leaky boat.'

'And it's getting dark,' piped my sister from the back seat. 'If it gets any wetter and any darker we'll be totally lost. If we're not lost already.' She leaned closer to Mum. 'Are we lost, Mum? We haven't seen a house or a person for miles and miles.'

Which was quite true. No twinkling farm-house broke the grey desert of night fields. No passing headlights touched us with the comforting evidence of other humans.

'We've done a quantum leap into the future,' went on Jo. 'Everyone's dead except us.'

Mum scowled in the gloomy light. Her ponytail had come undone and her hair hung untidily around her face making her look like an extra in a survival movie. She wiped the windscreen and then wiped her damp hand on her *Living Dance* tee shirt.

'Go back to sleep, Jo,' she said. 'The last thing I need now is your pessimism heaped on my head.'

Jo snorted and flopped back on the seat.

'I wish Dad was driving,' she growled.

I swung around and glared at Jo. 'If Dad was driving we'd be on the wrong road in the wrong county and probably stuck in a ditch.'

Jo made a grotesque face.

'That's a great improvement,' I scoffed. 'Though you don't have to work hard at it.'

'Look,' put in Mum. 'Are those gates ahead or am I seeing things? Cian, look at that map your dad sketched and see if we're close.'

I opened out Dad's spidery map and held it closer to the light from the dash.

'Well, that looks like the crossroads we passed about a mile back,' I pointed to a series of scribbled lines. 'And, if this is right, then they should be the gates of Glenderry House.'

I must admit to sounding a bit doubtful; I wouldn't trust my father's sense of direction to get me across our own yard on a clear day.

'Alleluia!' Mum sighed loudly. 'A cup of tea and a warm bed might just bring me back to life.'

'If there *are* beds and tea,' said Jo. 'Hasn't the house been empty for ages?'

I turned to glare again, but the car lurched as we hit a pothole and the moment was lost. We drew up outside the high, wrought-iron gates and tried to see along the overgrown avenue.

'It's spooky,' whispered Jo.

For once I had to agree with her. The territory beyond the comforting lights of the car was lost in wet grey and black shadows. The three of us fell silent for a few moments, listening to the rain hammering at the windows. Mum sighed and looked at me with that 'You're-a-great-lad' expression on her face. I knew what was coming.

'Better open the gates,' she said. Jo giggled.

'Why can't *she* do it?' I muttered. Let my pest of a sister be snatched into the darkness by whatever spooks were out there. She wouldn't be missed.

'You're the man in the family for the moment,' Mum said.

'Ha!' I'd heard that old chestnut many times before. Mum and Jo were big into the feminist thing whenever the equality of men and women was mentioned, but whenever anything involving sweat or courage was called for, they were your hysterical shrinking violets, and either Dad or I were saddled with whatever needed to be done. Like now.

'Maybe there's another way in,' I said hopefully. 'Maybe there's a back way with no gates to be opened.'

Mum's face hardened to a granite expression and I knew I'd lost that round.

'OK, OK,' I muttered before she could reply. 'I'll open the cruddy things.'

The icy rain made me catch my breath. I pulled up the hood of my anorak and dashed to the gates. They seemed even higher and more sinister from this angle. At first they wouldn't budge as I heaved and pushed.

'Put your back into it!' shouted a voice from the car. Smartass Jo.

I gritted my teeth and thought up ghastly ways of making her suffer as I pushed once more. The big gates finally yielded to my superior strength and, with a great creaking and squeaking, swung open. I sprinted back to the car, soaking wet.

'You're a great lad,' said Mum.

'Yeah,' I said, shaking my cold, wet hands. 'Great.'

The avenue was really long and twisting. High trees dripped eerily on either side. All the scene needed to make it the stuff of a cult horror were luminous eyes peering from the depths of the trees. I didn't look – just in case.

'I bet this is really nice in the daytime.' Mum tried to sound encouraging.

'How do you know if daytime ever reaches this creepy place?' I said. 'Seems to me that we've entered through the gates of hell. Dad was right. He told me years ago that he'd been here once or twice as a kid. He said that all he could remember was the dreariness. Glenderry Mausoleum he called it.'

'Thanks, Cian.' Mum gripped the wheel even tighter. 'Thanks a bunch for your helpful remarks. I don't want to be in this place any more than you do, but don't forget it's your—'

'Lights!' cried Jo.

'What!' Mum and I said together.

'There's a house ahead,' went on Jo. 'You can see the lights through the trees.'

Sure enough, between the wind-blown branches, we could make out the welcome signs of human habitation.

'Who'll be there?' asked Jo. 'Who'll be there to let us in?'

'Relations,' I said. 'All Dad's relations.'

'Nerd,' scoffed Jo. 'All Dad's relations are dead.'

'Exactly,' I smiled triumphantly. 'All Dad's dead relations are waiting behind the door to grab us as soon as we go in. They'll suck our blood and turn us into vampires. Though in your case there won't be any change.'

'Mum!' wailed Jo.

'Can it, Cian,' muttered Mum. 'Look, there's the house.'

The avenue divided in two around a big, circular shrubbery. On the far side of this, barely visible against the dark grey sky, loomed the house of my father's ancestors.

CHAPTER TWO

'Awesome,' said Jo.

We were standing in the open porch outside the big hall door. The ivy rustled wetly against the trellis on either side.

'There's a smell of damp,' said Mum.

'There would be, Mum,' I said with exaggerated patience. 'It's bucketing down out there, or hadn't you noticed?'

'No, not that kind of damp, cleverclogs,' she replied. 'Old damp. The musty, mouldy damp smell of old places.'

'Is someone going to ring the bell, or will we just stand here all night?' put in Jo.

'You're right,' said Mum. 'Here goes.' She reached up and pulled the ancient chain. Nothing happened.

'You've probably flushed the lavatory,' I said.

Mum snorted and pulled again. This time we

caught the faint peal of chimes.

'Wait for it,' I whispered to Jo. 'There'll be a shuffle and a couple of creaks and the door will be opened by a bony-faced weirdo with brain transplant scars.'

'You're the one who needs a brain transplant,' retorted Jo. But I was pleased to see that she was slightly scared.

'Stop being childish, you two,' hissed Mum. 'Remember this housekeeper is an old lady, so mind your manners.'

I did a little stiff-armed Irish dance in a puddle of rain that had settled in a hollow on the worn step.

'Riverdance,' I said. 'I'm a door-to-door Riverdancer with my own portable river.'

Jo giggled and Mum turned her eyes heavenward.

Then suddenly, we became aware of a shush-shush sound approaching.

'Listen,' I nudged Jo. 'Can you hear the shuffle?'

'Cian!' Mum growled.

Light flooded into the porch as the big door swung open. At first we couldn't see the face of the bulky figure who stood there, but when she backed into the light to let us in, we were met by a beaming, plump face. Not a scar or a brain transplant in sight. Major disappointment.

'You got here,' the woman smiled. Now here was one clever lady.

'No, no,' I said, forgetting Mum's dire warnings to be polite. 'Not at all. We're just figments of your imag—' I broke off as Mum squeezed my arm. Pinched, really. I made a mental note to add that to the list of grievances I was making for the cruelty-to-children people.

'Just joking,' I muttered.

The old woman laughed indulgently. 'I'm Mrs Barry and I'm delighted to see you. I was worried in case you might run into trouble in all that rain. They say on local radio that there's a danger of the river bursting its banks. They say that every time we have heavy rain but it hardly ever happens. Scaremongers, the lot of them. Take off your coats and we'll get you settled.'

She busied herself taking our coats and hanging them on the elaborate hall stand. The hall was big and cold with several doors off it. A wide staircase with good-for-sliding bannisters led up to a dark, railed landing.

'So, this is the O'Horgan heir,' Mrs Barry said,

switching her attention to me. Heir to what? Heir to this rambling old house in the middle of nowhere? Thanks a lot. I twitched a bit under her intent gaze. Mum coughed discreetly. Suddenly the old woman was all fuss and attention.

'You poor things,' she said. 'You must be frozen. Come on into the warm kitchen. I have a stew simmering on the range for you.'

She chattered away as she led us down a dark passage off the hall. Sure enough there was a comforting smell of stew. The warmth of the kitchen came to meet us.

The kitchen was a large, old-fashioned affair, the sort you'd see in films about olden times when men had hairy whiskers and women wore long dresses and stayed at home. The table was set for four. A basket of sweet-smelling rolls was in the centre. Mum slapped away my hand as I reached for one. I gave her my appealing, hungry waif look. A waste of time.

Mrs Barry shuffled over to the range and lifted the lid from the saucepan. Steam wafted around the kitchen as she stirred the stew.

'God knows what – or who – is in that cauldron,' I whispered to Jo. 'Toads' toes and rats' bellybuttons.'

Jo giggled and put her hand over her mouth.

'Sit yourselves down there and get dug in,' said Mrs Barry, lifting the saucepan on to a woven mat at the top of the table.

Several times during the meal I caught Mrs Barry staring at me. Was it my ears, I wondered? I instinctively felt them to make sure that my hair covered the tops of them. When I was younger I used to try sticking them down with chewing gum, which led to rows over gungy pillow covers. Letting my hair grow a bit longer did a much better job and, in a certain light, you wouldn't think I had sticky-out ears at all. But it wasn't my ears that Mrs Barry was looking at. Shoot, I thought, the old bird is doolally. Probably thinks I'm my own great-grandfather or some other old fossil from her past. Nevertheless, I felt uneasy. Nearly put me off my nosh. Only nearly.

'What's your room like?' Jo burst in as I was unpacking. She did a trampoline act on my bed, making the old springs creak. 'Not as soft as my bed,' she laughed. 'You could sink in my bed.'

'Why don't you do that?' I growled. 'Why don't you go and sink yourself out of sight?'

She stopped bouncing and stood looking at

me from the bed. Her fair hair was sticking up, making her look like a demented eleven-year-old punk.

'You're a miserable creep,' she said. 'You've done nothing but moan and grouch since we set out for here. I thought we could at least *try* to have a bit of fun. But not the great Cian – oh no. You have to play the grumpy martyr.'

She jumped off the bed and looked scathingly at me. 'You just can't take it, can you?' she cried.

'Can't take what?' I mumbled. 'What are you on about?'

'This house. You can't take on board the fact that I've been left money by the old great-uncle and you've been left this... this house.'

Now she'd hit a really sore nerve. That was exactly my major whinge; the loopy old relative had chosen *me* as heir to the family home. I ask you, what would I, a normal (if above average) twelve-year-old want with a mouldy old ruin in a nowhere place? It was too bizarre for words. I still harboured a hope that Jo, with her love of old places and things, would swap.

'How do you think Mum and I feel?' she went on. 'We don't want to be in this godforsaken dump either. I'd much rather be heading for

16

Killarney, like we'd planned. It's for your sake that we're here. Creep.'

She was absolutely right. I'd been behaving like a wounded cat since this trip was forced on me.

'Yeah, well,' I muttered. It wasn't exactly an apology, but it was near enough without choking.

'Well nothing,' put in Jo. 'Go and nurse your crabby face.' Then she flounced out of the room, slamming the door. Some flakes of plaster floated down from the high ceiling. I sighed and put on the old Meatloaf tee shirt I use for sleeping in. I was going to run after Jo to try and make some joke that would put me in a better light, but the effort was too great.

'Stuff everything,' I said aloud. 'And stuff washing,' I added when I discovered that the bathroom was at the end of a dark corridor. Besides, my hands had got pretty wet while I'd been opening the gates, so they were already washed.

The rain hadn't let up. It beat steadily against the window. Now and then the bedside lamp flickered and I held my breath in case the light went out altogether. I snuggled under the duvet and wished we'd never come to this creepy place.

Sometime during the night I woke up with a start. It took a couple of moments to realize where I was. The light was still on. I felt a bit spooked as I looked around to see what had wakened me. Apart from the rain which was still slapping the windows, the house was silent. The sort of silence that makes you feel extra isolated because everyone else is asleep.

It must have been the rain, I told myself. That cruddy rain which woke me up. That bit of reasoning gave me the courage to turn off the light.

But it wasn't completely dark. A bluish glow came from one of the windows. Must be nearly dawn, I thought. I peered at the luminous hands of the bedside clock. Three a.m. Hardly dawn yet. Anyway that glow was only coming through one window and not through the other.

I tried to ignore it, but I knew I wouldn't get to sleep again until I found out where that light was coming from. Perhaps old Mrs Barry liked to mooch about in the garden in the pre-dawn. Maybe she was digging somebody up, or putting somebody down.

'Get real, Cian,' I sniggered softly.

With a courage that surprised even myself, I

padded over to the window and eased back the curtain. My room was in the front part of the house, overlooking the big, circular shrubbery we'd seen on our way in. There was a blue haze coming from the shrubbery. The rest of the garden was in the darkness. I watched for as long as my courage lasted, which wasn't more than nanoseconds. But it was just long enough for me to feel that whatever was behind that dim blue light was staring at me, sizing me up. The back of my neck felt as if a thousand fleas on rollerblades were making their way up to my head. Heart in overdrive, I leapt to the bed and dived under the duvet.

'This cruddy place is freaking me out,' I panted to my knees which were pressed up to my chin. 'I wish that daft old man had dumped this pits of a place on someone else.'

CHAPTER THREE

'He was a real gent, your great-uncle,' Mrs Barry said. She was dishing up bacon and eggs to the three of us. 'A real gent.'

I wondered what an *unreal* gent would look like.

'Can I help?' asked Mum, looking uncomfortable as the old woman fussed about us.

'No, dear,' replied Mrs Barry. 'I've been doing this for over forty years in this kitchen.'

I don't know whether she was claiming her territory or being polite, but Mum didn't push any more.

'What was he like?' asked Jo, dipping her toast into the runny egg yolk. 'Great-uncle Cian, what was he like?'

'He was a real gent,' I put in. 'Isn't that right, Mrs Barry?'

If she realized I was taking the mick, she didn't

let on. Mum shot me a warning glance and I grinned at her. Her foot failed to connect with my leg under the table and she kicked the chair instead.

'And you've been his housekeeper all those years?' said Mum, with her eyes still firmly fixed on me.

'Aye,' smiled Mrs Barry, sitting down to eat with us. You could see she was a woman who enjoyed her grub, her wobbly chins proclaimed a more than passing interest in cream doughnuts and sugary apple tarts.

'And he never married?' asked Mum.

Mrs Barry looked up from the loaf she was cutting.

'No. No, he never married.'

'All his life in this big old house and nobody to share it with,' went on Mum.

Mrs Barry nodded.

'Except yourself, of course,' Mum said quickly. You could see that she was trying really hard not to put a word wrong. She was strangely ill at ease. But then there was a bit of a guilt trip involved. Apart from a card at Christmas, Mum and Dad had had very little contact with the late ancestor. Several times Mum had suggested that we should visit, but Dad had always made the same excuse.

'He's a recluse, Beth,' he'd say. 'He doesn't want visitors. The old fogey is as barmy as they come.'

Then Mum would look at Dad and nod her head. 'I can see the family resemblance,' she'd say. At which Dad would push his glasses along his nose and howl laughing.

So I'd never got to meet this great-uncle in the flesh. And now he'd popped his clogs and left *me* this gloomy place.

Of course it was Dad who should be here to sort things out, but he was on a lecture tour in America. If ever anybody could be recognized for what they do for a living, my Dad's job fits him like a glove. He is a professor of Celtic studies, and always has the appearance of a puzzled visitor to this century. Dad thinks Heavy Metal is ancient weaponry and that the Internet is something old women use to keep their hair tidy. He writes books on the Celts – big tomes of things which would fossilize your brain before you'd finished reading the title.

I take him with me to football matches in an effort to prove to the world that my old man is a regular sort. He does his best, but any eejit could see that he's like a dazed bluebottle in an ant farm – taking up space and wondering what's going on.

Between a far-out freak for a father, and a mother who teaches ballet to dumpy little girls in tights, I sometimes feel I got pretty ripped off in the parent market. I keep hoping they'll tell me I was adopted.

Dad has sandy-coloured, curly hair, the same as Jo's. He wears glasses which keep sliding down his bumpy nose. The bump was caused by his nose being broken when he was younger. I'd like to be able to say that it was the result of a good old ding-dong of a fight, but it was a revolving door that did it. Revolving doors tend to do that when you try pushing them the wrong way – ask my Dad.

When the letter had come to say that the house was left to me, I went ballistic with visions of coming to live in a swish mansion with a couple of servants and every comfort catered for. A man of property at the age of twelve. Quit school, kiss the folks goodbye and see them only at Christmas for the pressies.

It hadn't taken Mum long to put me right. The house wouldn't be mine until I was twenty-five for a start. Twenty-five! I'd be too old to enjoy it. Then she'd told me how old it was and, worse, where it was.

'I'll sell it,' I'd said. 'I don't want it. I want to sell it.'

The two parents had gone on about it being in the family for centuries and all that sort of heritage stuff, but the more they got their knickers in a knot, the more stubborn I got. It felt good to be able to say, 'It's my house. I can do what I like with it.' But I knew in my bones that I'd be lumbered with the old place.

That was when I'd started to get tetchy about the eight thousand pounds coming to Jo. And, now that I'd seen the house, I very definitely was not a happy bunny.

'Was it a big funeral?' Mum was asking Mrs Barry. 'We'd have come if we'd known...' Her voice trailed off. More guilt. This was great.

Mrs Barry stopped buttering her toast and fixed her eyes on Mum.

'What do you think, dear?' she said. 'The poor man shunned nearly everybody. No,' she went on with her buttering, 'he wouldn't have wanted a fuss. Just the priest and the doctor and some people from the publisher—'

'Publisher?' I interrupted. 'Was he a writer?'

Mrs Barry looked quizzically at Mum.

Mum leaned towards me. 'He wrote poetry,' she said.

'Ha!' I said with such force it hurt my tonsils.

'I like poems and rhymes and things like that,' put in Jo. 'But then, I'm blessed with culture.' She smirked at me. 'Dad says so.'

I fast-forwarded my brain to search for a suitable reply, but nothing came up so I just scowled.

'His books are in the study, Cian,' Mrs Barry said to me. 'If you'd like to see them.'

'Sure thing,' I said, pleased that she had singled me out. 'There's nothing I like better than thumbing through funky poems!'

Mrs Barry nodded. She looked like she was about to say something meaningful, but she pursed her lips as if to stop the words from coming out.

'Just look at that rain,' said Mum, neatly changing the subject. But a thought had suddenly occurred to me.

'Those books,' I said.

Mum turned to look at me, her expression not a million miles from disapproval born of suspicion.

'What about them?' she said.

'Well, you know those things that writers get when their books sell...'

'Royalties,' said Mum.

'That's the word. Well, who gets the royalties?' There might be some hope of a cash injection coming my way after all.

Mum gave a dry laugh. 'There's not much in the line of royalties from slim volumes of poetry. But what there is goes to Mrs Barry. Great-uncle Cian left the royalties and the rest of his money to Mrs Barry.' She looked across at the lady in question. 'And deservedly so for looking after him for all those years,' she added, just to show there were no hard feelings. None from her, at any rate.

Well, great, I thought. The old bird gets dosh and Jo gets dosh. Me? I get the short straw. It must have shown in my face. Jo slid her elbows towards me and put her face close to mine. The freckles on her forehead bunched together in a frown.

'I know what you're thinking,' she whispered as Mum and Mrs Barry moved on to make more banal conversation. 'I know exactly what's going through your nerdy mind and I think you're the most greedy, selfish pig I've ever met. Ever since we got word about the will, you've changed completely. I wish you weren't my brother. I wish the old Cian would come back. The fun one.'

'You don't know what you're saying—' I began.

'Yes I do. Our Miss Gahan told us that with some people, the more they get the more they want. You're one of them.'

'Mind your own business,' I said feebly. You'll always know a loser when he says that. And this time I knew I was a loser – in every sense. I hated to admit it to myself, but Jo was right. Things had got a bit out of proportion.

Jo slid back to her own place and looked at me triumphantly. To save face I mouthed something rude. Of course Mum saw.

'Come on,' she said, getting up and starting to clear away the breakfast things before Mrs Barry could stop her. As Jo joined her, Mrs Barry winked at me and beckoned for me to follow her from the kitchen. Goody. For some reason best known to herself, the old lady had taken a shine to me. No arguing with that.

'Hey!' called Jo, waving a tea towel. 'You're part of this too.'

'He'll only be a moment,' said Mrs Barry, ushering me out. 'He'd like to see the books.'

'I turned and grinned at Jo. 'Women's work,' I mouthed.

'Mum!' wailed Jo. But I'd gone before Mum noticed.

At first I couldn't see anything in the study, but when Mrs Barry pulled back the heavy curtains and let in the rainy daylight, I gasped. There were bookshelves lining all the walls from top to bottom. I'd never seen so many books in one room – and this from a lad whose father buys books like normal people buy shoes or ciggies.

'Wow!' I whispered. 'Did he write all of these?'

Mrs Barry laughed. 'No, dearie. Only those ones there.' She pointed to shelves behind the big desk near the window. 'He was a bit of a scholar, your great-uncle. Did all kinds of research and things like that. Brainy things.'

She stood in the middle of the floor, her arms folded. The carpet was faded and worn between the desk and the door. I could imagine the old man shuffling back and forth for years and years, wearing a threadbare track into the pattern. When I realized I was standing on the track made by the ancestral feet, I instinctively stepped to one side.

Mrs Barry ran her hand lovingly over the desk. 'These are all yours now, lad,' she smiled.

My jaw dropped. I had forgotten that I was a man of property, however reluctant, and that the property included the things in the house.

Mrs Barry reached into a drawer and took out a folder. She held onto it as if undecided about leaving it out or putting it back.

'This is his last work,' she said. 'He was writing this when I found him. The papers were scattered across the floor. I put them back in the folder and brought them here to the study.' She gave a sorrowful sigh. 'I know that's what he would have wanted.' She tapped it and left it on the desk. 'I'll leave you here to look round. Your great-uncle spent most of his days here. Look, you can see the rings on the desk from the many cups of tea and coffee I brought him. I know he'd love to think that you're here now, another Cian.'

Then she made her way to the door. Now, that prospect didn't fill me with delight. Being left alone in this room where the old geezer had died sent a shiver up my back. What was the old bird up to? Why dump me here among all these seriously boring books and then abandon me? I made to follow her, but then it occurred to me that if I went back to the kitchen I'd be roped into helping Mum and Jo. Better to twiddle my thumbs here for a while. I took a deep breath. The lingering smell of tobacco and old leather gave me the feeling that the dead relative could materialize at any moment.

'Nutter, Cian,' I said. 'Get real. The old man is dead and buried. End of story.'

I went to the shelves where great-uncle Cian's poetry books were displayed. One by one I pulled them out. It gave me a great buzz to see the same name as mine on the covers. I tried to imagine what it would be like if I were really the author.

The covers were really deadly – deadly boring that is. Thin books with unpronounceable titles, and lines of verse that didn't even rhyme. Mum was right, the royalties on this lot would bring in diddley-phut. I put them back and picked up the folder Mrs Barry had left on the desk. What great epic had the old man started before he snuffed it? To my surprise, it wasn't poetry. It was the beginning of a story. Great! This might amuse me until I was sure the washing-up was done.

It started with the blue light in the shrubbery, the

story began. That should have rung warning bells in my head, but it wasn't until the next bit that I freaked out. *Sometime, long after midnight, the blue glow reached my room. Thinking that the moon had at last begun to shine through the rain, I pulled back the curtain. But it was not the moon that caught my eye. It was the feeling of being watched, being scrutinized.*

That was it. I threw down the folder as if it was electrified. My feet were already on their way to the door.

CHAPTER FOUR

Mum and Jo looked up in surprise when I almost fell through the kitchen door.

'I'll put the dishes away,' I panted.

'What's brought this—?' Mum began.

'You're as white as a sheet,' put in Jo. 'You look like you've seen something scary.'

'No!' I growled. 'I've seen nothing. I've just come to help. Have you a problem with that?'

'No, no,' said Mum, wisely not questioning my sudden enthusiasm for work in case I changed my mind.

My hands were still shaking as I put the dishes away. It was only by concentrating hard on what I was doing that there weren't smashed plates and cups all over the floor.

'You want to play a computer game with me?' I asked Jo. *Anything* not to be left alone somewhere in this spooky house. 'I brought some games.' If only it would stop raining, then I could at least get out and breathe air.

'We're just going to sort through great-uncle Cian's things,' said Mum. 'See what we're going to keep and what we'll put into auction. You can help. After all, it's your stuff.'

That was another pain in the butt. The parents had decided, without even consulting me, that they'd auction off any furniture they didn't want to keep and put the money into a trust fund for my education. Education! I'd had enough of that, thank you very much. Far better to give me the proceeds and let me see the world. So, what a bummer – there would be one lot of money to put me through years of stuffy book-learning and then, at twenty-five, a dreary old dump in the middle of nowhere. Some prospect.

'Well?' Mum's voice brought me back to earth. 'Do you want to sort through things with us?'

I didn't want to touch anything that the old man might have touched. The very thought of it made the blood drain from my head again.

'Can you get it done quickly so we can get away from here?' I asked. 'I'm fed up already.'

Mum shrugged. 'It will take a couple of days.'

A couple of days! I'd be a gibbering lunatic by

then. I reluctantly watched them both leave the kitchen. Well, at least I'd stay here, it was warm and full of signs of human occupation.

'All on your own?' I leapt as Mrs Barry came in carrying some turf which she fed into the range.

'Imagine, it's the month of July and we still need to keep the range going.' She turned towards me. 'You didn't spend long at the books.'

'I… I wanted to help with the washing-up,' I stammered.

'Or was it that you read something that disturbed you?' she lowered her voice.

Keep calm, I said to myself. Unfortunately myself didn't listen.

'What do you mean?' My voice came out like a strangled screech.

'You looked a bit peaky when you came down this morning,' Mrs Barry went on as she wiped her hands on her big wrap-around apron. 'Is there anything you'd like to talk about, son?'

'No! No, I'm OK,' I snapped, relieved that my voice had come down a few decibels.

'That's good.' She opened a cupboard and took out a duster and some spray polish. 'I'll just be getting on with the dusting. If your mum is looking for me, I'll be in the drawing room. Switch on the telly there, if you like.'

'No, wait, Mrs Barry,' I said quickly. 'Don't... don't go.'

'What is it, son?' She came towards me and leaned on the table. I fiddled with the bundle of place mats. I noticed one of them had an egg stain. Probably Jo's. Suddenly I wanted, more than ever, for Jo to come and have some normal banter with me.

'Did something happen?' Mrs Barry asked quietly.

I nodded.

'Something last night?'

I nodded again. She sighed and sat down beside me.

'It's this time of year,' she said. 'It always happens at this time of year.'

I looked up at her and frowned. 'What happens at this time of year?'

'That blue light in the shrubbery. It starts with the blue light. It was that, wasn't it?'

I felt like I'd been hit with a concrete block.

'How do you know?' I asked. 'What's it about?'

Mrs Barry folded her arms across her cushiony

chest and leaned towards me.

'Have you wondered why this house has been left to you and not to your father?'

I shrugged. 'Not really. My Dad says it's because I'm called Cian, but that's a bit stupid. I think the old geez... the old uncle was gone a bit loopy—'

'Loopy, my foot!' said Mrs Barry defensively, her plump body wobbling with annoyance.

'I didn't mean...' I stammered. Me and my big mouth.

'Never mind,' Mrs Barry's voice became more soothing. 'The fact is that your father is right. It is because you're called Cian that you've inherited the house.'

I was about to say that I'd really have preferred the money, thank you very much, but I couldn't bear the thought of all that flesh quivering at me again.

'This house goes back to the seventeen hundreds,' she went on. 'The land itself, Glenderry, goes back to Celtic times, to the first O'Horgan chieftain.'

' A chieftain!' I exclaimed, brightening slightly. 'A chieftain called O'Horgan. Cool.'

'Not the sort of chieftain with feathers and a

teepee,' said Mrs Barry, misunderstanding my response.

I looked at her squarely. 'I know,' I said, with just the right note of scorn. 'I'm not a complete eejit, Mrs Barry.'

'Of course you're not, dear,' she patted my hand.

'Anyway,' I encouraged her. 'You were talking about the land.'

'Yes. Well, in the fifteen hundreds a bishop called Cian O'Horgan built a church here. When he died the land passed to his nephew, another Cian. It has been in the hands of a Cian O'Horgan ever since.'

'And now me,' I said.

'And now you,' she nodded. 'Your grandfather fell out with the family when he refused to call his son, that is your father, the family name, Cian.'

'Hang on until I work that one out,' I said. All these ancestors were scrambling my brain. 'Are you saying that the old man here never even spoke to my father just because Dad's name is Peter instead of Cian?'

Mrs Barry nodded again. 'Families are a funny bunch,' she said. 'Traditions die hard. But you are the heir and that's all that matters.'

The word 'heir' didn't sit comfortably on me. I felt like I should be wearing velvet drawers, and lacy stuff around my neck.

'Because I'm called Cian,' I said. What a drag! If I'd been called Fred I'd be at home playing soccer with my mates. I wondered whose bright idea it had been to give me the family handle.

'Is all this something to do with that blue light?' I asked.

Mrs Barry sighed heavily and put her plump hand on top of mine. Always a sign of trouble when someone tries to sound comforting before they drop a bombshell.

'It all goes back to Bishop Cian,' she said. 'He built his church and monastery on the site of a much earlier Christian community. It goes even farther back,' she leaned closer as if to drive this riveting fact home. 'The first O'Horgans were Celts who lived on this very spot. Of course they weren't called O'Horgan then, they took that name later on. Anyway, the ruins of Bishop Cian's church are just over the hill behind the house. He was a very powerful man and he was on good terms with the King of England.'

'England ruled over Ireland at that time,' I put

in, just to show that I had a brain in working order.

'Right,' nodded Mrs Barry. 'But then the King – Henry the Eighth – fell out with the church—'

I knew this bit as well. If you've got it, flaunt it. 'Because the Pope wouldn't let him boot his old wife and marry a new one,' I said.

'That's it,' she smiled approvingly at my show of knowledge. 'So then Henry decided to shut down the monasteries and take their land and treasures. He sent soldiers over to do that. The monasteries hadn't a hope against the might of the army. Many of them were plundered and left in ruins.'

'And Bishop Cian?' I asked.

'Well, when he heard that the soldiers were coming, he made the monks dress like peasants and sent them, with the valuable books and things, by sea to France.'

'And what about himself?' I asked. After all, the man had my name, why wouldn't I be extra curious?

'He stayed,' said Mrs Barry. 'He resolved that his land would never pass into the hands of the King, that it would always be O'Horgan land. He

39

had deeds drawn up, making the land over to his nephew—'

'Don't tell me,' I put in. 'Another Cian O'Horgan.'

'Another Cian O'Horgan,' she laughed. 'Even though his mother was married to someone with another name, she reverted back to O'Horgan when he died shortly after the boy was born.'

'How do you know all this?' I asked.

'Your great-uncle had to unburden himself on someone,' she said. 'He was a lonely old man who had so much on his shoulders.' She paused and looked towards the window.

I wanted to ask what was on his shoulders but decided that, maybe, I didn't really want to know.

'Anyway,' she looked at me, 'to get on with the story. Bishop Cian kept the most valuable thing in the monastery and hid it where it would never be found by the soldiers.'

My ears pricked up. 'What valuable thing?'

Mrs Barry paused for a moment. Then, almost in a whisper, she said, 'The Glenderry Goblet.'

'A goblet.' My antennae waved. 'Do you mean something valuable like the Ardagh Chalice?'

Hidden treasure. Riches.

Mrs Barry shrugged. 'Who knows?' she said.

'Nobody has ever found it.'

'Has anyone ever looked for it?'

She smiled uncertainly. 'Oh yes. It has been looked for over the centuries. It has been looked for by more than the living.'

I felt a serious illness coming on. 'What do you mean?'

CHAPTER FIVE

Mrs Barry looked out of the kitchen window again, as if seeking inspiration from the rain clouds that rolled overhead.

'The Glenderry Goblet was very old even then, in the fifteen hundreds,' she said. 'It dated back to when Christianity first came to Ireland, and had actually been in the family for centuries. The bishop treasured it.'

'So he buried it?' I said impatiently. 'Go on.'

'He *hid* it. Nobody knows if it was buried, but it would seem the obvious thing to do. Bishop Cian knew that the King's army wouldn't spare him. "When I die," he said to the faithful young monk who'd insisted on staying with him, "you must bury me in the grounds of my church. And you must promise, when it is safe, to retrieve the goblet and put it with my bones. It must never fall into the wrong hands." '

'How do you know that they were his exact words?' I asked. I must say I found it pretty ludicrous to hear this plump little old lady spouting words from an eminent ancestor of mine. 'Wouldn't he have used old-fashioned words like *thee* and *thou*?'

Mrs Barry looked at me and snorted. 'I'm telling you all this exactly as your great-uncle told it to me,' she said. 'And he got it from his ancestors. This story has been handed down for generations.'

'And how did the bishop know that this other monk wouldn't snuff it first?'

Mrs Barry shrugged. 'Will you let me get on with the story?' she said.

'Sorry.'

'Well, the army came,' she continued. 'The bishop met them at the door of his church. He told them that he'd sent his monks and the church valuables to France, otherwise the soldiers would have ransacked the village looking for them. The captain was a ruthless man. He had been garrisoned locally years before and knew of the precious Glenderry Goblet and how important it was to the bishop. He refused to believe that the bishop had sent it from this country to France, so he was determined to find it – not for the King, but for himself.'

'And did he tell? Did Bishop Cian tell?'

'Of course not,' said Mrs Barry, in a tone that made me regret even asking. 'Not a dickybird. In a rage, the captain sacked the church and had the bishop put to death.'

'How did they kill him?' I asked eagerly.

Mrs Barry looked at me. 'Gory little beggar, aren't you?' she said. 'They chopped his head off, if you must know.'

'Oh, wow! That's cool.' I was awe-struck. Here was another relation to boast about – one who'd had his head lopped off. These ancestors were an amazing lot.

Mrs Barry shook her head in disapproval.

'I mean… I mean he was pretty brave,' I added hastily. 'So, did the monk do as he was asked? Did he retrieve the goblet and put it with the bishop's bones?'

'That's just it,' said Mrs Barry. 'It seems the poor devil did a runner when he saw the troops coming. It was the locals who buried Bishop Cian in the burnt-out ruins of his church – his tomb can still be seen there. They knew nothing about his wish to have his treasured goblet buried with him.'

'So it was never found?'

'No. Never found,' went on Mrs Barry.

'So how did the bishop's wish become known?' I asked. 'If he was dead and the monk had scarpered, how did it become known?'

Mrs Barry brushed a couple of crumbs off the table on to the red-tiled floor. She sat back in her chair and looked at me. 'Many years later,' she continued, 'the monk came back to fulfil the bishop's wish. He told the story to the nephew who was living on the land by then, and they both searched for the goblet. The land layout had changed. There was no longer a community of monks, so the nephew had built a substantial farm house with outbuildings. The monk had no idea where the goblet was. It never turned up. The bishop's wish was never carried out.'

She stopped. I felt that creepy feeling that was becoming pretty familiar by now. We looked at one another in silence for a few moments. I noticed a nervous tic in one of Mrs Barry's eyes. There must be heavy stuff to come, I thought, as I swallowed hard.

'The old parish annals show that the sacking of the church and the bishop's death took place

45

around the nineteenth of July,' she said eventually.

'Nineteenth of July?' My voice had gone all screechy again. 'That's… that's—'

'That's tomorrow,' said Mrs Barry. 'And,' she sighed and added, 'it's also the anniversary of the death of your poor great-uncle.'

That was about right, I realized. It had been about a year ago that we'd heard that the old man had shuffled off. We had just come back from holidays in Scotland and we heard that he had died a few weeks previously. We had thought no more about his death until a couple of weeks ago when a solicitor's letter came to the house. It had taken ages for the will and all that legal stuff to be sorted out.

'Are you going to tell me that every Cian O'Horgan dies on the nineteenth of July?' I asked.

Would I get to see thirteen?

'Not at all,' replied Mrs Barry. 'Just coincidence.' But her words didn't inspire me with positive thoughts.

'And that blue light?' I continued, my heart now in overdrive. 'That thing that I saw last night, and that great-uncle Cian saw too?'

'I don't really know,' she replied to my unspoken question. 'I just know that, at this time every year, your great-uncle would become pale and gaunt. There were always signs, when I'd come up to clean, that strange things had been going on.'

'What kind of things?'

'Things pulled about. Oppressive atmosphere,' sighed Mrs Barry.

'Sounds just like my bedroom,' I said, in a pathetic attempt at a joke. She didn't laugh.

'And the old man would just sit staring into space and rocking back and forth,' she went on. 'I used to feel so sorry for him, so helpless.'

'That light,' I began. 'Could it be the monk, the one who scarpered, coming to look for the goblet?'

Cripes, was I really having this off-the-wall conversation?

She shook her head. 'I don't think it's the monk,' she said. 'I've never seen it – your uncle would never let me stay over, even though I wanted to help him – but from what he told me I know that it's too… too evil to be someone who means well.' She paused and massaged a bumpy finger. 'Too evil to be a man of God.'

'Oh jeez!' I exclaimed, jumping up. 'I've got to get away from here! This is too freaky.'

Mrs Barry put out her hand and stopped me in my panicky tracks.

'You can't,' she said simply. 'You must pick up where your great-uncle left off.'

'What do you mean?' I tried to pull away from her.

'Only a Cian O'Horgan can lift the curse…'

'No way!' I yelled. 'I want to go home. Muummm!'

But Mrs Barry was holding me fast by the arm.

'The sun never shines on this house,' she raised her voice against my gibbering protests. 'Apart from trees and a few shrubs, nothing grows. This house and land will stay dead until the promise is fulfilled.' She stopped.

'Get away from me!' I yelped. This was serious freak-out time. Knees, voice, bones, everything was trembling with the spookiness of it all. 'I'm not staying here. I don't want this cruddy house – I never wanted it. You can have it.' I broke away and ran towards the door.

'It's no use,' cried Mrs Barry. 'The commitment is yours now. It's all on your shoulders. You're the owner of the house, you have to see the promise through. It doesn't matter where you go, the commitment is yours.'

That stopped me in my tracks. I turned to look at her. Her face was white and anxious. My own face must have been green; at least it felt like that from the inside.

'That goblet must be found and buried with the bishop's bones,' she said. 'And only you can do it.'

'I'm twelve years old,' I protested. 'I'm just a kid. I couldn't be expected—'

'You're old enough,' said Mrs Barry.

'No!' I was desperate now. 'What if I just go away and never come back?'

'Your life wouldn't be worth living.' She looked at me pleadingly.

'Old great-uncle Cian did all right for himself,' I muttered. 'He became a writer, even if it was only poetry.'

'Your great-uncle was a lonely old man. He was troubled all his life by this commitment, as were all the ancestors who lived here.'

'Why didn't he just go away?' I was having difficulty trying to make sense of this. 'Why didn't he pack his bags and scarper?'

'He did! He travelled all over Europe, but

everywhere he went he was haunted by the pull of this place.'

'Oh cripes,' I said. How could I become a famous rock star or astronaut with this spooky stuff dogging me? I felt my legs give way and I slid to the floor.

'What'll I do? What'll I do?' I wailed. I really wasn't feeling very well.

'Look for the goblet,' said Mrs Barry, coming towards me. She stooped and patted my shoulders.

'Mrs Barry.' I tried to sound reasonable, but my voice was still wobbly and screechy. 'If all the ancestors tried and didn't succeed, what chance have I? I wouldn't know where to begin.'

She cupped my face in her plump hands. 'You must try, lad,' she said. 'I'll help.'

'Thanks a bunch,' I muttered. Great, a skinny kid and a fat old lady would succeed where generations of O'Horgans had failed. The image of the two of us sitting on a JCB ploughing up the land didn't smack of optimism. I wished my father was here.

'Does my father know?' I asked.

Mrs Barry shook her head.

'Nor Mum?'

'You're the only one,' she said. 'Your father's father tried to suppress it – that's why he gave your dad a different name. He thought if he told nobody, the scourge would simply go away. He felt it wouldn't touch his side of the family – after all, your great-uncle was living here at the time. Perhaps he thought the old man might still marry and produce his own heir. Or perhaps he'd intended to tell your father sometime, but your grandfather died while still quite young. No, you and me, we're the only ones who know the story now.' She looked upwards to where muffled chatter was coming from upstairs. 'Do you think your mother and sister could handle all I've told you?'

I tried to think like an adult – a difficult thing to do as I often find it hard to think like a twelve-year-old.

'Mum wouldn't believe a word of it,' I said. 'And Jo would freak out. Maybe I'd better keep this to myself for a while.'

Mrs Barry straightened up. Outside, the rain was still beating against the kitchen windows, making me feel more isolated than ever. I got up and tested my legs to see if they were still working.

'Brave lad,' said Mrs Barry.

Brave? I've known sick rabbits with more courage than I was feeling just then.

The cheerful voices of Mum and Jo coming down the stairs brought a welcome sense of reality. Mrs Barry set about filling the big kettle.

'A cup of tea, I think,' she said. Her cosy tone made me wonder if this was the same woman who had been frightening the bejapers out of me for the past hour or so. Cups of tea, spooks and headless bishops didn't gel somehow. My head was really messed up.

'There's loads of interesting stuff up in the attic,' Jo burst out enthusiastically. 'You should see it, Cian. It's deadly.'

'Yeah?' I tried to sound enthusiastic too, but I'd aged about ninety-five years since I last saw my sister.

'It's going to take ages to sort through everything,' said Mum.

'Take as long as you like, dear,' said Mrs Barry as she scooped tea from a battered tin and put it into a round teapot with blue flowers painted on it. 'I'm delighted with the company.'

I bet she was.

'Have you always lived here, Mrs Barry?' Jo

asked, reaching for the plate of flapjacks Mrs Barry had put on the table.

'Heavens no, lass,' she laughed. 'I live down in the village. On my own now, of course. Husband died twenty years ago and my two sons are in America. I used to come up here every day on my bicycle. Now, since Mr O'Horgan died, I've been coming up to air the place. Except for now, of course. I'm staying here at the moment to give you a hand and to see that you have everything you need.'

'That's very good of you,' muttered Mum.

'Not at all,' went on Mrs Barry. 'I like to be here. People say it's a gloomy old house, but you know,' she gestured around the warm kitchen, 'I quite like the old place.'

'And now you'll have loads of money,' went on Jo. 'Mum says that you looked after our great-uncle very well and that you deserve all the money he left you. He left me some too. Isn't that nice? What will you do with yours, Mrs Barry?'

'Really, Jo,' muttered Mum. I hadn't the spirit to gloat at her embarrassment.

Mrs Barry smiled. 'I might go to America for a while, and visit my sons,' she said. 'I've always wanted to see America.'

Mum had gone over to the window. She wiped the condensation and looked out.

'That's really bad,' she said. 'I don't know when I last saw rain like that. It makes everything so gloomy, so eerie.'

I wanted to burst out with my awful news, to hear my mother say soothing things like, 'Don't be daft.' But something deep inside told me that wouldn't solve anything.

CHAPTER SIX

'Do you want to come up to the attic with me, Cian?' asked Jo, wetting her finger and gathering up the remaining crumbs of flapjack. 'It's brilliant old stuff. Really old. You wouldn't believe how old some of it—'

'No, I don't want to go.' I tried not to sound scared out of my mind. All I wanted was for all of us to stay in the kitchen until such times as we could go away from here. I wondered if I should pretend to have taken on a sudden fever or an agonizingly tortuous bellyache that would mean a prompt cheerio to this place and its ghouls. But Mum would recognize the symptoms – I'd tried that once too often before maths tests.

A sudden crash from upstairs made us all start.

'Oh cripes!' I muttered. My heart had been doing so much thumping over the past hour or so that my blood didn't know if it was coming or going.

'It's all right.' Mrs Barry laughed and looked at me as if she knew the state of my nerves. And so she should, she was the one who'd stirred them up. 'It's only the landing window. It does that sometimes in a strong wind. I'll fix it.'

'I'll go,' said Mum, getting up. 'I'll see to it, Mrs Barry.'

But the old woman was on her feet.

'Not at all, child,' she said. 'I know how to secure it tightly. Me and that window have been fighting for years. I have the measure of it.'

I waited until Mrs Barry had left, then I leaned across to my mother.

'Mum, can we go soon?' I whispered hoarsely.

'There's so much to sort out—' began Mum, looking at me with surprise.

'I know, I know,' I said urgently. 'But can't we come back later? September maybe?' That should give the spook time to get back to his mouldy grave.

Mum laughed. 'Cian, if I didn't know any better, I'd say you were frightened.'

A voice within screamed at me again to tell her everything, that her earthy logic would scoff at the whole bizarre story. That we'd laugh at it, the three of us, and put it down to an old woman's ramblings. But it wasn't as simple as that.

'Frightened? Me?' There was that screech again. 'Nah, just bored.'

Mum pursed her lips and nodded. 'That figures,' she said. 'But don't forget, young man, that the only reason we're here is on your account. This is your house and—'

'I know,' I held up my hands. I didn't need reminding of that grotesque fact.

'I like it here,' said Jo. 'I think it's great. There's loads of interesting stuff.'

'Can it, Jo,' I mumbled. If I could have stormed to my room I would have. But fear clamped me to my seat.

There was a thump and a clatter from above, followed by a pained cry.

'Mrs Barry!' shouted Mum, on her feet and rushing to the door, closely followed by Jo. And me. I wasn't about to stay anywhere on my own.

Mrs Barry was lying in a heap at the foot of the stairs. One foot was twisted under her. Mum ran to her and cradled the old woman's head.

'Are you all right, Mrs Barry?' she asked.

What a daft question, I thought. Any fool

could see that the old woman was in a mess. Mrs Barry raised her hand. At least she was alive.

Mum was looking at the ankle. 'You poor dear,' she said. 'That looks very sore. Don't try to get up.' She looked up at me. 'Cian, phone the hospital, quickly. Jo, get some blankets.'

The number was written, along with other emergency-type numbers, on a card pinned over the phone. I gave the details to the nasal female at the other end.

'Both ambulances are out,' she said helpfully. 'There's been an accident, what with the flooding and all—'

'This is an emergency,' I shouted. 'Can't you get somebody out here?'

'I'm afraid it will be about an hour before they're back,' said Nasal Nellie.

'Well, thanks a bunch,' I muttered. I called out this information to Mum who was wrapping the blankets Jo had brought around Mrs Barry.

'An hour!' exclaimed Mum. 'We've to wait an hour?'

Mrs Barry clutched at Mum's arm.

'No time,' she whispered. 'Heart. I have a heart problem. Need to get to the hospital. Please. Straight away.'

Mum looked concerned. 'Yes, of course,' she said. 'I'll drive you there. Come on, kids, give me a hand.'

With much heaving and pushing, the three of us succeeded in getting Mrs Barry into the back of the car. Her face was deathly white and I wondered if she'd make it the twenty miles to the hospital.

'We'll squash into the front,' I said.

Mum looked at me as she got into the car. 'What?' she said.

'Jo and me, we'll squash into the front.'

'Don't be daft,' said Mum. 'We don't need a whole procession going to the hospital like a circus parade. You two stay here. I'll be back as soon as Mrs Barry is settled in.'

'What! Stay here? Mum!' I stuck my head in to plead with her.

'Go on back in out of the rain,' called Mum, starting the engine. 'I'll be back as soon as I can.'

Mrs Barry was scrabbling at the seat to get my attention. 'The soldier,' she wheezed. 'Cian, lad, watch out for the soldier. I should have told you, but I thought I'd be with you...' Her voice trailed off as the effort got the better of her. She sank back in the seat, her eyes still on me.

'The poor dear is rambling,' Mum murmured to me. 'Must hurry.'

I looked towards Mrs Barry again. Her eyes were popping as she tried to communicate with me.

'What soldier?' I almost shrieked. 'What soldier, Mrs Barry?'

'Where I found your uncle,' she gasped. 'Find the san—'

Mum leaned across and pulled the door from my grasp. 'Rambling,' she said again, and slammed it shut.

'Oh help,' I moaned as the car sped down the avenue. I stood watching, not even noticing the rain that was soaking every part of me.

'Why are you standing there with your mouth open?' called Jo from the front door. 'You look like a fish.'

Right this minute I'd settle for being a fish, I thought. Happy and spook-free, swimming up and down with other fishy things. I looked up at the house and shivered, before resigning myself to going in.

'Will you come up to the attic now?' asked Jo.

'Let's just watch telly,' I said, switching it on.

'It's only half-three!' cried Jo. 'There's only

old people's stuff or kids' programmes on now.'

'There might be an old movie. Let's get some of those flapjacks and watch an old movie.' I was almost grovelling. I'd have watched a party political broadcast on behalf of the Suit and Dandruff party – anything to show that there was a real world out there.

As it happened, there was a very old musical on called *Brigadoon*, with men in skirts and girls with lurid lips singing and leaping around a bunch of cottages. Just the sort of stuff to send my fingers to my throat in the days when I had a life. At least it kept Jo in the kitchen, and I pretended to enjoy it with her. I even kept her supplied with orange juice and goodies.

'What's wrong?' she asked.

'Wrong?' I paled. Was there something behind me? I was afraid to look.

'You're being so nice,' went on Jo, dipping a flapjack in the juice.

'Don't push your luck,' I tried to growl, but it came out as a whisper. Whimper, more like. I was really screwed up.

CHAPTER SEVEN

When Jo fell asleep on the big, lumpy sofa in front of the telly, I turned the sound down. Not out of any consideration for her, but as long as she was asleep she wouldn't be wanting to mooch about the rest of the house in pursuit of more 'old stuff'. I kept glancing at the window, waiting for the crunch of wheels on the gravel. The loud ticking of the age-browned wall clock seemed to mock me over the muted music from the telly.

Tick tock, tick tock, the rhythm of the clock, along with the beating of the rain against the window, took over my whole body and I found myself rocking back and forth in time with the sounds.

The soft chimes of five o'clock died away. They had been gone an hour and a half, Mum and Mrs Barry. Keep your head, I tried telling myself. After all, it would take the best part of an hour to get to the hospital on these unfamiliar roads and in this rain. And it would take another while to get Mrs Barry settled. I shouldn't expect Mum before half-past six at least. To keep my mind from dwelling on Mrs Barry's last, cryptic words before Mum swept her off, I concentrated very hard on a programme about the many exciting uses for old milk cartons. But it didn't work. What was the old woman on about? What soldier? And what about the place where she'd found my great-uncle? Why had she used the word 'san'? What was 'san' – Santa Claus? Sandbank? Sanitation Department? 'Forget it. Mum was right, she was rambling,' I whispered to myself.

Half-past six came and went. So did half-past seven and half-past eight. Even though it was July, it grew quite dark. I turned on the light and did a bit of channel-surfing. There was nothing on that would relieve my anxiety. I looked at Jo, still curled up at the other end of the sofa, and envied her. If only she knew what a terrified nerd her brother had become. On the one hand I wanted her to stay asleep so that she wouldn't sense my nervousness; on the other hand I could have done with another human voice to keep me sane.

'Come on, Mum,' I whispered.

The sudden ringing of the telephone startled us both. Jo blinked and looked around her, for a moment unsure of where she was. She yawned and stretched. One side of her face was red and had the bobbly pattern of the cushion imprinted on it.

'That's the phone,' she looked at me with a puzzled expression. 'Aren't you going to answer it?'

'Of course I am,' I said. It was good to hear human sounds again. I jumped over the back of the sofa and grabbed the phone. It was Mum. I felt a flood of relief.

'Are you on your way home?' I asked.

There was a pause before she spoke.

'You could at least ask how Mrs Barry is,' she said with a tinge of disapproval.

'What? Oh yeah. How is she?' I know I didn't sound convincing, but then, they say that self-preservation is the strongest instinct and right now I was deeply into self-preservation.

'Her ankle is just sprained, but they're keeping her for a couple of days on account of her heart condition. She's comfortable now, the poor dear. In fact she's asl—'

'Good. That's great, Mum. So, you're on your way then?'

'Well, that's what I'm ringing about, Cian,' went on Mum. 'It seems the river has burst its banks and the Glenderry side of the hill is completely cut off. The police tell me that there's no way I can get back until tomorrow.'

'What! Tomorrow?' My voice was strangled. 'You can't mean it, Mum! You can't be serious. You've got to come back.'

'Cian!' Mum's voice broke in. 'I'm sorry. There's nothing anyone can do. Don't you think I've tried? I asked if there was any bridge farther down, but they tell me that road is notorious for flooding. The house is frequently cut off. All we can do is wait.' She paused again. Surely she could hear my heart thundering. 'I told the police and the firemen that I had to get back, that my two children were stranded in Glenderry House—'

'What did they say?' I interrupted her. 'Can't they get a helicopter or something? Mum, we can't stay here, Jo and me. We can't.'

'Cian,' Mum tried to sound soothing. 'It's only

until tomorrow. The fire brigade will be able to pump the water away tomorrow.'

'Why can't they do it now?' I wailed.

'Glenderry House is on a hill,' she reasoned. 'There are other houses in danger of flooding in the valley. They have to get priority. Can't you understand that, son?'

'So we've to spend the night here on our own?' I was practically gibbering by now.

'That's not such a big problem, is it? I'll be along as soon as it's possible tomorrow.'

'Oh, Mum,' I groaned. I wanted to scream into the phone and tell her about the spooky blue light and the way Mrs Barry had messed up my head, but there was no way those words would come out and make sense. By now Jo was twitching beside me, beckoning for me to give her the phone.

'Cian,' Mum was saying. 'Be adult about this. Don't make me feel bad when you know there's nothing I can do. You're both old enough to be able to look after yourselves.'

I'd heard enough. I handed the phone to Jo and threw myself onto the sofa. Through the mist of my misery, I was scarcely aware of the animated conversation between Jo and Mum.

'Don't worry about a thing, Mum,' Jo was saying. 'We'll be fine. Tell Mrs Barry we said hi and that we hope she'll be OK again soon. See you tomorrow. Byeee.'

She put down the phone and turned towards me.

'You prat,' she said. 'What did you want to give Mum all that grief for? There's nothing she could do. What do you want? Have her swim across the river to be with her little darlings? Get real, Cian.'

'You wouldn't understand,' I muttered.

'I understand OK. I understand that you're a selfish pig. You never wanted to come here and now you're doing the martyr.'

'I'm not,' I protested feebly. 'I just...' I trailed off. How could I begin to tell Jo about the whole spooky thing? Maybe if I didn't think about it nothing would happen. Maybe Mrs Barry was just a dozy old lady who'd spent too many years looking after my weird great-uncle. I cheered up slightly. That was it, the poor old dear had let the old man's imaginings go to her head.

I held on to that thought.

'What do you say we fry up some sausages and pig out, Jo?' I tried to sound cheerful.

'I'm too full,' said Jo, still frowning. 'I ate too many flapjacks. Maybe later. I'm going back up to the attic. I've found loads of things up there. You should see it. Mum says that anything that's sold will be put in trust for you. That means—'

'I know what it means,' I put in. 'I get pushed into some nerdy university instead of joining a rock group.'

Stuff the whole inheritance thing, I thought. I'd happily dump house and money if I could just go home.

'So, are you coming with me?'

'Where?'

'To the attic. To look at the old stuff.'

I sighed. If it was a choice between that or stay here on my own, I'd opt for the attic.

'OK,' I said reluctantly. 'Just for a while.'

I followed Jo as she bounced down the hall towards the stairs. This is what's real, I kept telling myself. Me and Jo sharing something like we normally do. Life is normal. There's no such thing as spooks.

I had almost convinced myself when the lights flickered for a moment and then went out.

CHAPTER EIGHT

'Hell,' said Jo.

I didn't say anything. I couldn't, because I was choking with terror. I clutched at the bannisters and held on for dear life.

'This is mega scary,' went on Jo. Her hand felt my shoulder. 'Ha, there you are, Cian. As usual it's me who's scared of a little bit of dark. I wish I was as casual as you. Here, will you hold my hand?'

I gladly held on to her hand, squeezing it so that she wouldn't feel how much my own hand was trembling.

'I know where there are candles,' she said. 'Mum and I came across a whole box of them today. They're in the dining room, just off the hall. Let's go back down, come on.'

I croaked 'OK,' then cleared my throat and

said it again with a bit more control. I really didn't want to move. I wanted to cower where I sat until Mum came. But Mum wouldn't be back until tomorrow. Now would not be the time to tell Jo about my session with Mrs Barry. But then again, Jo is a pretty balanced kid for her age, I reasoned. Maybe if I told her she'd laugh and restore me to normal and we'd both have a good giggle.

I sighed and reluctantly let go of the bannisters. Jo led the way downstairs in the smothering dark.

'I'm glad you're with me,' she said. 'I'd die if I was here on my own.'

'Jo,' I began. I couldn't keep up a pretence of bravery any longer. I wanted Jo either to share my scare or else scoff it away. 'Jo, there's something I want... something I have to tell—'

At that moment the front door burst open and a gust of rainy wind blew into the hall. Jo screamed and threw herself at me, burying her face in my neck. As I looked, gobsmacked, towards the door, a faint blue glimmer appeared for a second and disappeared down the hall. But it wasn't so much the dim light as the warm, cloying heat that followed it, a suffocating heat that was filled with threat and menace. I unlocked Jo's hands from around my neck.

'It's in,' I whispered. 'Oh God, it's inside the house!'

Jo held on to my sweater. 'What are you saying?' she asked. 'What's inside the house?' Her voice rose into an angry hysteria. 'This is not the time for putting the frighteners on me, Cian. Don't do this.'

'The rain!' I said hastily. 'The rain's come in. Come on, let's get that door closed before the hall gets soaked.'

She was almost dragging me as we felt our way to the door. Together we slammed it and pulled the old-fashioned bolt across. It struck me then that I had done this before. And I had. After Mum had driven off and I'd come back into the house, I had definitely pulled that bolt across.

'It's so hot,' Jo was saying. 'The hall is like a hothouse after that. Can you feel it, Cian? And the stink. Yeeccchhh. The sewage must have burst.'

I shivered. There was indeed the most awful stench, worse than filthy socks and mouldy cheese which had been left in a plastic bag for a week. It was the sort of smell that went through every pore of your skin and made you gag. My mind was a quivering mess by now. How could I begin to tell my scared sister that things were a hundred times worse than they seemed? At least she hadn't seen the light.

There and then I resolved to try and put on a brave face. It was either that or be dead jelly. 'Let's get these candles,' I said with a calmness that would win an Oscar. 'You lead the way, Sis, I don't know where this dining room is.'

Still clutching my hand, Jo led the way across the wide hall and groped at a door. A different smell of damp and polish met us as she opened it. And cold. The cold coming on the heels of the sudden heat was teeth-chattering.

'This is it,' she said. 'Over this way. There's a whole box of candles in the sideboard over here.'

It suddenly dawned on me. 'I've no matches!' I exclaimed. 'We've nothing to light them with!'

'It's all right,' Jo laughed nervously. 'There are matches as well. Mum says that they must be used to having their electricity knocked out, there are so many candles. Ha, here we are.' She let go of my hand and pulled out a big box. We felt around inside it and, sure enough, there were neat bundles of candles stacked together. Jo rattled a box.

'See? Matches.' She sounded relieved.

'Light all of them,' I said quickly. Any longer in this mind-scrambling darkness and I'd turn idiot.

'All of them? Shouldn't we keep some for later?'

'Stuff later,' I replied. 'It's right now we want the light. Give me some of those matches and we'll put candles everywhere.'

The warm glow from the candles took some of the eeriness away, but I was still very conscious of that blue glimmer that had vanished into the hall. Maybe it was just a trick of the light from outside, I told myself. But I'd been *trying* to tell myself so much of late, that myself had gone deaf. There was no way I wanted to leave this room and venture back down the hall.

'Let's stay here,' I suggested. 'We'll leave all the candles lit and stay here. We'll put a chair against the door, fasten the shutters and snuggle under the table. There are probably tablecloths and stuff in a drawer, we could make a nifty tent.'

Jo was looking at me, her candlelit face filled with amazement.

'What are you on about, Cian?' she asked. 'Stay here all night? Have you not noticed how cold it is? All the tablecloths in the world wouldn't keep us warm in this icebox. No, we'll go back to the kitchen. The range is going full blast, that'll take the chill off us. Let's take these candles down to the kitchen.'

'You mean, go back down the dark hall?' I gulped.

'Well it won't be dark if we're carrying candles will it, silly?'

I shivered, both from the cold and from fear of what was beyond the hall.

'We'll carry two candles each,' suggested Jo. 'Blow out the rest and we'll take them with us to the kitchen.'

As soon as we ventured out into the still-cloying hall, Jo's candles immediately went out. She'd been carrying one in each hand and so they weren't protected from the current of stinking, warm air. Because I'd had the foresight to carry both together in one hand, I was able to cup my other hand over the flames. Although they flickered and wavered, they stayed alight until we got to the comfort of the kitchen. Once there, we lit most of the rest of the candles. I took Jo's advice and kept some aside, just in case. We pulled the lumpy sofa closer to the range and heaped it with cushions.

'This is fun, isn't it, Cian? Will we stay here all night and not go to bed at all?'

'Why not?' I agreed, not letting on that that was my idea all along. There was no way I was going to be alone tonight. All I wanted to do now was to bury my head under the cushions and not surface until daylight. But Jo had other ideas.

'What'll we do now, Cian?' she bounced up and down, causing the nearest candles to flicker. 'There's no telly and no radio, so what will we do? Will we play I Spy or something? Cian? Cian? What are you looking at? Are you trying to scare me again? I'll scream—'

'Did you see that?' I whispered. That glimmer had briefly passed the door, its blue light showing in the small gap between the bottom of the door and the floor.

Jo clutched my arm. 'You stop that now, Cian O'Horgan—'

'Ssshhh,' I whispered. 'Don't say my name, you clown!' I didn't want that... that thing to know my name.

'I'm going to tell Mum,' went on Jo. 'I swear

I'll tell Mum that you spent your time scaring me to death. You're so mean. I wish you were dead.'

She just might get her wish, I thought.

There it was again! The blue glimmer flickered past the door once more. I froze. This time Jo saw it too. We watched with fascinated terror as the light hovered at the door. The warmth from the range was replaced by the suffocating heat we'd felt in the hall.

'Cian!' exclaimed Jo. 'What's out there?'

The stillness of the dim glow was scarier by far than its movement. For a heart-stopping moment, we held on to one another. But Jo decided she had had enough.

'Get out!' she screamed. 'Go away, you nasty thingy. Leave us alone!'

That's done it, I thought, with the small part of my brain that was still working. Prepare for the fingers of death on your throat, Cian. In an instant, the glimmer was gone. The kitchen returned to its comforting atmosphere again.

Jo turned towards me. She was shaking.

'What did you do?' she asked.

'What do you mean?'

'How did you do that? What did you rig up to scare me?'

'Me? I didn't do anything. That... that's part of this house.'

'What?' She clutched herself and leaned closer to me. 'What are you on about?'

So I told her. There was no point now in trying to hide anything from her. Besides, she'd seen the thing for herself.

She looked at me, her face pale, her eyes and mouth wide open in amazement, as I told her all that Mrs Barry had told me.

CHAPTER NINE

'Jeepers, Cian,' Jo whispered when I'd finished. 'What'll we do?'

I shrugged. 'I don't know,' I admitted. 'I just want to get as far away as possible and never come back to this place.'

'But you can't,' she said, with her usual practical outlook. 'If Mrs Barry said that this... this haunty thing will follow you everywhere, like it followed great-uncle Cian and all the other ancestors—'

'I know, I know,' I put in. 'But I'd happily take my chances if I could just get away.'

'Well, we're stuck here for the night,' went on Jo.

'Thanks for reminding me,' I muttered.

'Could *we* look for that goblet?' she asked.

'Jo,' I tried to sound reasonable. 'If every one of our ancestors looked for the bloomin' thing, what chance do you think we'd have?'

Jo sank into a thoughtful silence. Outside, the rain continued to beat against the window, adding a rhythm of fear to this eerie situation. Is all of this really happening? I wondered. How can life suddenly turn into such a nightmare? It didn't make any sense. Please God, could I please rub out today and start again? Start by not coming to this ghastly place. I wished I'd never heard of Glenderry House. Above all, I wished my parents had named me Fred.

'Maybe if we followed that... that blue thing,' Jo was saying.

I looked at her in disbelief. She was supposed to be scared silly and here she was suggesting that we follow a spook.

'You've got to be kidding,' I said.

'No,' she reasoned. 'It might just lead us to the place where the goblet is hidden. It might not be able to retrieve it because its hands would go through it or something. Do you see what I mean?'

Well, that certainly made sense, but I shuddered at the thought.

'I think we should leave things alone,' I said.

Jo shook my shoulder. 'Hello,' she said.

'You're not listening. Either we find this goblet or you'll be spooked for the rest of your life.'

Now I was really sorry I'd told her. I'd been afraid that she'd turn into a hysterical lump, but instead she was suggesting brave deeds that were too far out for me.

'Let's just sit here,' I said.

'Cian!' she shook my shoulder again.

No sooner had she done so than the smothering aura pressed around us once more, giving us the feeling of being bathed in rotten, warm syrup.

'There it is,' whispered Jo, pointing towards the dim light under the door. It was as if that thing was poised outside, listening to us, sizing us up like it had been sizing me up last night. Maybe if we stayed very quiet it might get fed up and slither back to where it came from.

I swore inwardly when Jo broke the silence. 'Blast it! I've had enough of this.' There was no fear in her voice, just determination.

I moved closer to her, trying not to cry out. I marvelled at her calmness and tried to put on a brave face. Still, I'm never one to take chances with matters spooky, so I stayed well down in the sofa.

'Now,' said Jo as the light began to move again. 'Come on.'

'No,' I pulled back. 'Leave it, Jo.'

'Well I'm not going to sit here like a scaredy-cat all night,' she declared. 'I'm going after our friend here. Are you coming or not?'

This was not my kid sister talking, I thought. Something has possessed her, just to add to my already full list of problems. I'd heard about people being possessed by evil. They ended up spewing green gunge and making furniture hop about. Yet, deep down, I should have known that Jo is a gutsy lady when the chips are down. And now the chips were as down as they could be. I took her outstretched hand and we eased our way across the kitchen. Very slowly. I didn't want to get too close to that thing.

Jo looked at me.

'Here goes,' she said, opening the door.

The thunderous roar that met us drove us both back with cries of terror. The door crashed against the dresser, causing some plates to smash. I lost my grip of Jo's hand as the roar completely surrounded us, blowing out all the candles. There was no blue light now, just that threatening presence that seemed to sweep me up in a black stranglehold.

'Jo!' I screamed. 'Jo!'

'I'm here, Cian!' Her voice seemed to come from a distance.

I stepped in the direction of her voice, but my foot made no connection with the floor.

'Jo!' I was falling, like in one of those dreams you have after a late-night Chinese takeaway where you feel yourself falling and wake up with a bump. Only this time there was no comforting bump. I was dizzy and still falling.

The roar had changed to a thundering sound that got louder as it drew closer. I shook my head and then clapped my hands over my ears. There was shouting. Was it me? No, my mouth was clamped shut with tension. It wasn't Jo. It was men. Lots of men shouting. The darkness was dissolving into a grey light. The thundering sound came from galloping horses. Horses? In my great-uncle's hall? But I wasn't in my great-uncle's hall, was I? Was this some sort of virtual reality thing? No, there was nothing on my head. Where was my sister?

I tried to call out, but no sound came from my mouth. Now the grey light was clearing. A stone church was silhouetted against the sky. Two figures stood at the door. The taller one had his arms folded across his chest, a grim look on his face. Standing beside him was a woman in a long dress. Her fair hair hung down in a single plait. I seemed to float closer to the two of them. With a jolt I recognized something about the man. Yes, he was dressed in priestly clothes, but it wasn't that that made me start.

He's got my ears! I thought. This man is wearing my ears, the O'Horgan sticky-out ears. This must be Bishop Cian!

'Stop!' He held up his hand to the horsemen. 'This is sacred property. This is the house of God. Go in peace and leave us alone.'

'We are here on the orders of his majesty King Henry,' boomed a voice. No matter what way I twisted I couldn't see the face of the speaker. But his voice was full of hatred and menace, hatred and menace that were familiar because it was the same hatred and menace that pervaded the kitchen and hall. I tried to cover my face, but my hands wouldn't move.

'There is nothing here for you, Grimstone,' said my ancestor. 'Your family have tried for years to wrest our treasured goblet, but it will never fall into your corrupt hands. My monks have left.

They have taken the sacred articles with them. There is nothing left but the church.'

Grimstone. Now there was a name to inspire fun happenings.

'Search this place!' Grimstone shouted to his men.

There was a clatter of hooves as the riders forced their horses past the bishop and the lady, and entered the church. The captain leaned threateningly towards the bishop, but I still could not see his face.

'The goblet,' he said in a low voice. 'Tell me where the goblet is.'

The bishop shook his head. 'It is not here, Captain Grimstone,' he said, giving a scornful emphasis to the word 'captain'.

Grimstone moved his horse forward. 'I know that goblet will never leave this land,' he said, his voice deep and threatening. 'You have said so, many times, I am told. Tell me where it is.'

'Why don't you go away?' The lady stepped towards him courageously.

I gasped when she stepped into the light.

'Jo!' I tried to call out. 'Jo!' How could my kid sister be standing there giving lip to some mediæval thug? 'Jo, get away!' I tried to shout again, but no words came out. But was it Jo? My sister was an eleven-year-old kid, this was a grown woman. But she had Jo's features and Jo's hair. This was too much. I couldn't take any more. I tried to pinch myself out of this nightmare, but like everything else, my fingers didn't work either.

'Leave my brother in peace and go back to your king,' the woman was saying. 'There is nothing to be gained from persecuting us. Only damnation.'

'Guard your tongue, madam,' snapped the captain. 'I am a soldier of the King and I demand the respect due to my position.'

Soldier? Captain! Of course! This must be the soldier Mrs Barry spoke of. This was the evil she was warning me of. I wanted to see his face, to know what it was I was up against in this whole terrifying nightmare, but his back was all I could see, the shapeless black of his cloak that draped over him like a flapping shroud.

'Tell your brother to obey me, lady,' he continued.

'Never!' snapped the sister. 'Leave now, you instrument of the devil. Leave before damnation claims you.' She had thrust herself in front of her brother and looked up at the captain.

'You anger me, shrew,' snarled the captain and, reaching down, he lifted the sister by her plait. At that, the bishop sprang into action. He tried to pull the captain from his horse, but was kicked to the ground. I was flailing about with my fists and trying to cry out, but it was as if I wasn't there.

'Burn this place!' shouted the captain, still holding the sister so tightly by the hair that she couldn't move.

'Jo!' I tried, furiously, to kick my way out of this paralysis, but still nothing worked.

With savage whoops, the soldiers lit torches and threw them into the small church. Within moments it was a blazing inferno. The flames were reflected in the chainmail and armour of the soldiers. Two of them leapt from their horses and grabbed the bishop by the arms. All the while I was shaking with frustration. There was nothing I could do. Why was I here if I couldn't help? What craziness had brought me here and why?

'For the last time,' the captain, whose face I still could not see, shouted to the bishop. 'Tell me where the goblet is and I will spare you.'

But the bishop shook his head.

'That goblet will never fall into your evil

hands,' he said quietly. 'Its double powers will rest with my bones.'

Making a superhuman effort, the bishop's sister twisted her head around and sank her teeth into the captain's wrist. With a roar he released her and, as she ran towards her brother, he took out his sword, swung it over his head and, with one quick blow, he killed her. Killed her! Right there before me. It was as if I was watching my own sister's death!

'Jo!' I cried out, my head bursting with frustration, but no sound came. The bishop rushed to her body, his face filled with grief. He lifted her head and stroked her forehead. Then he looked up at the captain, his face white and calm.

'She was young,' he said. 'She was a widow who now leaves an orphan son, my nephew. It is to the boy that this land will pass, not to your avaricious king.'

He gently laid his sister's head on the ground and stood up. With great dignity he looked straight at the captain.

'You will never rest,' he said quietly. 'Your soul will find no refuge until my bones and the bones of my sister are laid to rest with our sacred goblet. And when that act is fulfilled,' he pointed a finger at the captain, 'your soul will be banished to a netherworld of evil where it belongs.'

There was a frenzied roar from the captain. He lifted his bloodstained sword.

'You've breathed your last, priest,' he snarled.

Just before the fatal blow was struck, the bishop turned his head and looked straight at me. I blinked, but there was no mistake, he was looking straight at me, his ears – replicas of my own – framing his white, gaunt face. He gave a very slight smile and nodded. And then I knew what I had to do. I knew that, of all the family ancestors who had come since that time, it was I who had finally to break this curse. I was the one who must banish the captain's menacing spirit from this place.

'Yes,' I shouted. My voice, suddenly finding sound, echoed eerily. 'I'll do it, Bishop Cian. I'll do it!'

He nodded again and looked at peace. My last sight of him was as he knelt to receive the blow from the captain's sword.

The scene faded. 'I'll do it,' I said again. This time my voice sounded normal. Do what? What on earth was I to do? And Jo. Jo! I suddenly remembered my sister and realized that she was in great danger. The evil presence that had thundered into our great-uncle's hall was Captain Grimstone. For some reason much deeper than I could then understand, I knew he would rest at nothing until he'd located the goblet. And Jo was now part of all this too.

CHAPTER TEN

It was the musty smell of damp mixed with lavender polish that told me I was back in the hall. It took me a few moments to get my head together and to realize that the smothering warmth was gone.

'Jo!' I called out. My voice echoed in the pitch darkness. Strangely enough it was not the thoughts of spooks and spirits that filled me with terror right now. It was my concern for Jo's safety.

'Jo!' I cried out louder.

I could have wept with relief when I heard a soft groan coming from the direction of the stairs. I groped my way across.

'Ouch!' exclaimed Jo as I stepped on her toe.

I sat down beside her and held on to her. 'You're alive!'

'Of course I'm alive, you great twit! I must

have passed out or something,' she muttered. Her elbow hit me in the face as she raised her arm to rub her head. 'I feel like a rag doll that's been left out all night.'

'Are you OK?' I asked. I was so glad she was alive I was saying all the obvious, inane things. They say the brain goes like that in times of catastrophe. Someone is pulled, bleeding, from a crashed plane and some idiot will say, 'Are you OK?' Answer: 'Yeah, sure I'm fine. Is that my leg over there?'

'My hair,' Jo went on. 'It feels like someone's been trying to pull it out by the roots.' I felt her turn towards me. 'Were you trying to pull me along by the hair?' she asked.

My blood turned to frozen yogurt. I couldn't even answer.

'Well?'

'Jo,' I began.

I heard her sigh shakily. 'It wasn't you, was it?' she said in a low voice.

I shook my head. When I realized she couldn't see me in the dark, I said 'No,' hoarsely.

'Come on,' said Jo. I sensed her getting up. 'Come on back to the kitchen and we'll light the candles. If we sit here any longer in the dark we'll go bananas.'

Once again her calmness amazed me. It was as if some outside force had put a big chunk of courage inside her head. I got up and followed her, shivering slightly.

'I'll hold your hand,' I said.

Happily the kitchen had remained warm. I wondered why it stayed so normal in this ghastly house. Perhaps it had something to do with the fact that it was Mrs Barry's domain. She had nothing going for the ghoulish Grimstone so maybe he left her quarters alone. I hoped.

We quickly relit several candles. Jo sat on the arm of the sofa and I perched uneasily on the edge.

'It's not over yet, is it?' she asked.

I shook my head miserably. 'It'll never be over,' I mumbled.

Jo bounced off the arm and landed beside me.

'We'll make it be over,' she said.

'How?' I asked, conscious now of the promise I'd made to Bishop Cian and feeling useless because I knew I was powerless.

'There must be something...' began Jo.

'Jo.' I looked at her, my jaws barely able to move with the tension that was crushing my whole body. 'You're never going to believe this, but someone, or something has given me a glimpse of the past. I know what happened.' I stopped to see if she was going to scoff, but her face was serious.

'Go on,' she said. 'The way things are going I'd believe anything.'

So I told her of the sacking of the church and the killing of Bishop Cian and his sister.

'The murdering yobbos,' she whispered when I'd finished. 'If I'd been there—'

Her eyes widened and she put her hand to the back of her neck. 'I was there,' she said slowly. 'I felt I was there. What you're saying happened to you – I think I was part of that, but everything seems like a dream that I can't remember.' She paused and looked thoughtful. Then she shook her head. 'No, just a haze,' she said. 'But I know, in my head, that there's a heavy scare and that we're in it up to our necks.'

'Put that to music and you could sing it,' I muttered.

'That... thing. That stinking, warm thing,' continued Jo. 'Is that the soldier? Is he the one who killed the bishop and his sister?'

'Guess so,' I replied. 'He's after the goblet.

He's trying to prevent it from being reunited with the bones of the bishop.'

'Because then he'll be banished to hell,' put in Jo.

I nodded. 'Something like that.'

'Do you believe in hell, Cian?' asked Jo.

I looked at her. 'Believe in it?' I said. 'We're in it!'

'Dad says it's not about fires and demons,' she went on. 'He says it's a netherworld where people's own evil swallows them in a black grip for ever.'

'Yeah, whatever,' I mumbled.

'So, no wonder that captain is trying to make sure the curse put on him doesn't come true. To think that he's the one who's put all our ancestors through so much misery all these years. We're back to that goblet again, aren't we, Cian?'

I nodded. 'I don't know what to do, Jo,' I said. 'I promised, but I don't know what to do.'

Jo sighed. 'I wonder if there are any books in the study that would tell us anything.'

'Tell us what?' I looked at her.

'Tell us about this goblet, what it looks like and all that.'

'Don't you think that everyone who's searched

94

before us would have gone over that?' I said. I lit another candle to make the place a bit brighter. 'Anyone worth their salt would have been through the books. Except...' A thought had suddenly struck me.

'Except what?' Jo leaned closer.

'Except that today, in the study, I found a manuscript – more of a diary really – that great-uncle Cian had begun just before he died.'

'What did it say?'

I shuffled a bit. 'Dunno. I threw it down and ran.' I waited for a sneering response to that, but there wasn't one.

'Then let's go and look.' She jumped up, causing the candles to flicker.

'What? No more heroics, please.'

'Let's go and read this diary, it might tell us something.'

'But it's in the study,' I cringed.

'Yeah. So? Are you just going to sit here all night and wait for that... that evil prat to scare the life out of us? Ha, well, I'm not! Come on.'

Of course she was right, I knew that. But that didn't stop the yellow streak of cowardice from becoming an all-over pattern on my panicky body.

Jo was gathering candles.

'Are you sure you want to do this, Jo? This is spooky stuff.'

Jo's eyes glittered with scorn in the candlelight.

'All right,' I said. 'Just don't come running to me when all hell breaks—'

'As if,' she scoffed. 'Shut up and come on.'

We held our breath as Jo opened the door. I'd have done it, but I was standing behind her. There was no thunderous roar, just the eerie silence of the black hall.

The way my heart was thumping against my ribcage we might as well have had a Lambeg drum beating time as we made our way to the study.

'Here we are,' I whispered when we reached the study door.

The manuscript lay where I had dropped it, its pages scattered across the threadbare carpet.

'He didn't write very much,' said Jo, holding the candles as I gathered up the sheets.

'He died,' I said. 'Mrs Barry said he died before he got very much written.'

Jo took the papers from me.

'It started with the blue light in the shrubbery,'

she read aloud.

'I know,' I snorted. 'I read that bit. I'm not a complete fool.'

Jo read on and turned the page. I shuffled about and peered into the eerie shadows being cast around the room.

'Let's take it back to the kitch—' I began.

'Ha!' said Jo, pointing to the page she was on.

'What?' I leaned over her shoulder.

'Listen to this,' she said. '*And now, at the end of the twentieth century, I find I am the one to resolve this horrendous haunting of our family, the O'Horgans...*'

'What? Let me see.'

'Thought you'd read it.'

'Missed that bit,' I muttered. 'Go on, what's next?'

We both leapt as that thundering roar suddenly broke the quietness again and sent its menacing vibes into our bones. This time it was coming from upstairs. It sounded like furniture being flung about. Jo and I clutched one another.

'Oh no,' I groaned. 'I wish I could go unconscious and wake up when this is all over.'

'Under here,' said Jo, grabbing my arm.

'Where?'

'The desk.'

She was already easing herself under the kneehole part of the huge desk. I squeezed in beside her. We huddled together as the thundering above reached a crescendo.

'It's coming down the stairs,' I whispered.

Jo blew out the candles.

'What the hell did you do that for?' I blinked in the sudden darkness.

'No point in drawing attention to ourselves,' she whispered.

'That... thing doesn't need candles to tell it where we are,' I hissed.

How right I was. No sooner had I said that than there was a loud rumbling outside.

CHAPTER ELEVEN

We shrank back as far as we could into the kneehole, every muscle tensed, waiting for the door to burst open. If it wasn't for the fact that my fist was firmly stuck in my mouth, I'd have been screaming like a banshee with piles. The rumbling was replaced by loud banging. He's taunting us, I thought. He'd no trouble getting through the bolted front door, so why make a display of trying to break into the study? What was his hellish little game?

I squeezed Jo's arm.

'He's trying to break our spirit,' I whispered. 'He's trying to scare us so badly that we won't fight him.' And succeeding, I thought. Personally, I felt I was as much use as cold tapioca and probably looked worse.

Jo didn't hear me. I nudged her and felt that she had her hands over her ears. Ears. Ancestral ears. I focused my mind on the bishop who'd sported my ears and I was overcome with a sudden surge of loyalty and courage. It didn't last long; the door handle rattled, I closed my eyes and prayed for a sudden death – or any other form of unconsciousness.

The noise stopped suddenly. The silence was deathly. What next?

'Is it gone, do you think, Cian?' whispered Jo.

"Ssshhh, don't use my name!' I said. No point in advertising me like live bait. 'He might just be biding his time.'

'Biding his time?' she hissed. 'Ghouls like that don't know about time!'

We sat huddled together for another while, until we both began to twitch with aching muscles.

'I think it… he's gone,' said Jo. 'Let's get out of here.'

'And go where? We're safe here.' The small hidey-hole was giving me some comfort, a sense of security against whatever was out there in the open spaces of the old house. At least in here there wasn't room for a ghoul.

'Don't be daft,' said Jo. 'It's cold and cramped. Let's go back to the kitchen. Then we'll be able to read this diary and see what's to be done.'

Dammit. Why couldn't she just be scared like any normal kid? She was already out on the floor. Her absence left a cold gap beside me. I could hear her rubbing her legs.

'Come on,' she muttered.

'I'm just lighting a candle,' I retorted with an I'm-in-charge voice.

Sticking very close together, we crept out into the passage. Nothing charged at us, no black shape hurled itself at us, but my nerves were on panicky standby anyway. We eased our way back to the kitchen without mishap. It was still warm and some candles were still burning. Jo bounced onto the sofa and took the manuscript from under her sweater.

'Here, you read it,' she said. 'It's part of your stuff. Read it out loud.'

'Where did we stop?' I asked.

Jo pointed with a grimy finger. 'That bit where it says: *and now, towards the end of the twentieth century, I'm the one to resolve this awful curse against the O'Horgans.*'

'He resolved it?' I hadn't taken that bit of information on board first time round. I peered closer.

'Does that mean—'

'That he found the goblet?' Jo looked at me, her eyes wide.

I put down the papers. 'Could he have? After all these years?'

'Go on, read some more,' put in Jo.

'Yeah, right,' I cleared my throat and took up the next paragraph.

'*For so long the evil greed of Captain Grimstone has haunted and almost destroyed our family. A greed which has driven his exiled spirit to search for the sacred object, the precious Dual Deity Goblet which, should he possess it, will give him power over the Forces of Evil.*

So many times have I, and those who went before me, tried to document the awful events which dogged the very life of this ancient clan. But the written word was denied us; each time one of us tried to write about the horror which followed us, that very horror pervaded every corner of the house and every pore of the writer until the exercise had to be abandoned. Captain Grimstone – for it was he, always he – was determined that no documents would exist in this house which would aid an O'Horgan to locate the Dual Deity Goblet. The story had to be handed down by word of mouth, the burden passed from Cian to Cian.'

'What does Dual Deity mean?' put in Jo.

'I'll work it out later. Will you let me go on?' Jo nodded.

'*Until now*,' I quoted with just the right dramatic note. '*This very day I have at last found that precious object, the Dual Deity Goblet.*'

'He *did* find it!' whispered Jo.

'*Over the centuries our ancestors believed it to be buried here in the tribal land. The blue light which emerged with chilling persistency from the shrubbery was thought to mark the spot, but no amount of excavation would ever reveal the object or banish the evil. No amount of exorcism would ever bring flowers, sunshine or birdsong to this desolate spot. No amount of running away would ever give peace to the current incumbent.*'

'What's an incumbent?' asked Jo.

'I think it means whoever owned the house at the time. Whoever has charge over the estate,' I replied, glad that I knew something she didn't.

'So, you're the incumbent now,' she went on. 'You're the Cian who owns—'

'Will you give over,' I growled, glancing around to check that there was nothing lurking in the shadows, listening, targeting me and my cruddy name for a personal assault of the demonic kind. 'Don't interrupt.'

'Sorry. Go on.'

'How heartbreaking then to discover that, through all the centuries the sacred goblet was concealed all the time here in Glenderry House! It was purely by accident I happened upon the safe place. Here now I write. I've taken chair and trusty old typewriter and now I can write down all that has befallen our family. I wait until dawn, when my action will finally lay to rest this evil scourge.'

'What?' said Jo. 'The goblet's been here all the time? But where?'

'Look, do you want me to read this or not? We'll come to it.'

Jo wriggled impatiently beside me.

'To begin at the beginning,' I went on. I glanced at Jo. Her lips were firmly clamped together to stop more questions coming out. *'To begin at the beginning, it is necessary to understand the nature of our ancient people, the Celts. Last year I visited Professor Ethan Evans, an expert on Celtic history.'*

'Like Dad—' began Jo.

I ignored the interruption *'Together we searched through ancient manuscripts to see if there was any reference to this part of Ireland. On the third day we struck gold – we found a tenth century document which briefly referred to this site. Here, on this hill, the founder of what was to become the O'Horgan clan established his farm community. His tribe had come to Ireland from Gaul to escape the Romans in around 50 AD.'*

'What's all this to do with the goblet?' Jo asked impatiently. 'Can't you skip ahead to the bit about the goblet before that... that thing comes back?'

She had a point. I tried picking out the important bits that might lead us to the information we needed right now.

'It goes on to say that the clan held out against all invaders right up to the time that Christianity came to Ireland in the fifth century. Ah, listen to this:

'In the early days of Christianity, a monk by the name of Giraldous came and founded a monastery on the far side of the hill, on the land donated by the O'Horgans. For many years the community of monks and the clan of the O'Horgans lived side by side. There was always a son of the clan who would join the monks. The coming of Christianity to Ireland was a peaceful event. The Christian religion was merely absorbed by the people who did not greatly move away from their old ways, customs and—'

'And art,' interrupted Jo.

'I looked at her, gobsmacked. 'How did you know…?'

She grinned. 'I read Dad's books,' she said. She would, little Miss Know-all. 'The Celts just used the same kind of art that they'd always used, all those curly patterns and little square men with egg-shaped faces. Except that now they used it on chalices and high crosses and stuff like that instead of on pagan stones and jewellery. Now, are we getting to the goblet bit?'

I nodded and read on.

'To celebrate the first O'Horgan clansman to be made a bishop in the sixth century, the chieftain had his craftsmen remodel an ancient druidic goblet by adding Christian motifs to the pagan ones which already decorated it…' I paused as realization dawned on me. 'Dual Deity!' I exclaimed. 'That's where it comes from!'

'What do you mean?'

'Dual means two. Deity has something to do with gods. Don't you see? The goblet belongs to two religions – Pagan and Christian. It's a mixture of both!'

'Wow!' whispered Jo. 'So that's it. That's why it's special.'

I picked up the pages again.

'*That goblet was used as a chalice by the monks at the abbey right up until the sacking of the monasteries by King Henry the Eighth. It was known to be a priceless work of art, not just because it was fashioned from Irish gold and was highly decorated, but because it was believed to carry the combined powers of Celtic druids and Christianity – a Dual Deity that brought with it all the benevolence of good living. The area around Glenderry was renowned for its peace and beauty – the glen below the hill was rich with oak trees, hence the name which in English means the Glen of the Oaks.*

The O'Horgan lands were rich and fruitful, the monastery was a place of pilgrimage and learning which was protected from invaders by the mighty O'Horgans...'

'Until fat old Henry the Eighth sent his heavies,' put in Jo. 'How did he know about the goblet?'

'No, it wasn't Henry,' I said, glancing at the words ahead. 'It was Captain Grimstone. Listen to this:

'*Professor Evans very kindly did some further research to try and locate information about Grimstone, whose dreaded name had been handed*

107

down by word of mouth from O'Horgan to O'Horgan. Professor Evans contacted a colleague who is Lecturer in Mediæval Studies at Cambridge University. He faxed us back his appalling find.'

'I don't want to know about mediwhatsit stuff,' Jo interrupted. 'Get back to the goblet and the O'Horgans.'

'Wait. I'm coming to all that. Can't you keep quiet until we get the whole story?'

'It *is* quiet now, isn't it, Cian? Everything is quiet.'

She was absolutely right. I'd been so engrossed in what I was reading, I'd almost forgotten the earlier horror. The only sound we could hear was the drip drip of the rain from the trees outside the window – normal sounds.

'It doesn't even feel creepy any more,' went on Jo. 'It must be over. The haunting must be finished for tonight.'

'Hope so,' I said, afraid to let myself be too optimistic and yet trying to hold on to the thought that our ordeal might indeed be over. 'Maybe you're right. Maybe his batteries have run down.'

Jo gave a great sigh. 'Well, we got through it,' she said. 'Who'd ever believe—'

'Mum will,' I put in. 'Mum will be back tomorrow and we'll tell her everything. Then we can leave this blasted—'

Jo was shaking her head. 'You have to sort it out, Cian. You know that. You said yourself you can't run away from it. We have to sort it out now, you and me. I couldn't go through another night like this.'

I made a face. No point in arguing with my stubborn sister, but in my own mind I had decided on a prompt exit at the first light of dawn. 'I suppose,' I fibbed. 'We'll read on and piece things together.' The fact that the terrors of the night had apparently ceased was very comforting, like someone throwing a blanket around you after you've been rescued from the river. I picked up the manuscript again.

'Grimstone,' prompted Jo. 'You were at the part about Grimstone.'

I began to read again:

'*Captain Grimstone was descended from Godfrey Grimstone, a crusader who went to the Holy Land in the eleventh century with a Norman knight called Tancred. With a band of their own crusaders, they broke into a Moslem temple and ransacked it. As well as the valuables which he brought back, Grimstone*

also *hacked off a piece of what is known as the Rock.
This is the Rock from which Mohammed rose to
heaven and it is sacred to the Moslems.*'

'So, he took a bit of rock,' scoffed Jo. 'What's
all this to do with anything?'

I ran my finger down the print. 'Here it is.
Listen: *Because he had served on several missions to
Ireland, the crusading Grimstone was aware of the
Dual Deity Goblet of the O'Horgans—*'

I get it!' Jo cried. 'He had this bit of rock that
was sacred to the Moslems and now he wanted
the goblet as well.'

'To put them together and have a Triple Deity
Goblet,' I added.

'Which would give him supernatural power,'
went on Jo. 'The clever monster.'

I looked at the pages again. 'It says here that
for the next five hundred years, Grimstone's
descendants tried in vain to get the goblet from
the O'Horgans.'

'And we know the rest from whatever
happened to us earlier on,' Jo said in a reverent
whisper. 'The murder of Bishop Cian and his
sister.'

'That's it,' I agreed. 'Cripes, this is heavy stuff,
Jo. I don't know if I can take it all on board. My

head's a mess.'

'Yeah, well it never took much to do that. Is that all that's written down?'

I ignored her insult with dignity. 'There are two more pages,' I said huffily.

'Well, go on then.'

'*Shortly after Captain Grimstone had sacked the monastery on the hill and murdered the bishop and his sister, he himself succumbed to a mysterious illness which ate at his flesh and drove him insane. It was from then that the great shadow of evil spread itself over the O'Horgan clan. For all these years, Captain Grimstone's restless spirit has continued to seek the Dual Deity Goblet. To possess it, and incorporate into it the piece of the Rock of Mohammed, would give him power over the Force of Darkness, power that would undo much of the good on earth, power that would crush many religions and render them useless, power that would create greater evil in this world than man could ever understand.*'

I looked at Jo. 'And I'm supposed to sort all this out?' I put down the sheets of paper. Dawn was now too far away for my intended flight. 'Let's talk about real life, Sis,' I said, with a quake in my voice. 'Let's just get up nice and quiet, head for that back door and run like the clappers down to the village. I'm out of here. You can call me all the names you like, but I'd much prefer to take my chances out in the real world.'

'I won't call you names,' said Jo. 'I'm scared too. But I'd be far more scared if I thought this Grimcreep was going to haunt you for the rest of your life. I'm in this too. You don't want to end up a scared old man with big ears, afraid of the dark – afraid of everything. I'll help you, Cian. Here,' she picked up the pages, 'there's just a little bit left. Listen.'

I perched on the arm of the sofa as she began to read.

'Today, acting on a million-to-one chance, I uncovered the Stars and the Sword. Of course it all made sense – the Stars of Christianity to guide and the Sword of Cian of the Tuatha de Danaan to protect.'

'The who?' My turn to interrupt.

This time it was Jo who knew the answer. 'They were the people of the gods of Dana,' she said. 'Gods who floated through the air to settle in Ireland. Dad told me about them. They go back long before the Celts. So does your name. See? It says *Cian of the Tuatha de Danaan*. You're called after an ancient god.' In spite of the awesome situation we were in, she sniggered.

'I'd still prefer to be called Fred,' I muttered. 'Go on.'

Jo continued reading.

'*And thus I found the sanctuary which has remained hidden since this house was built around it. It was here that Bishop Cian placed the precious goblet under an unmarked little slab all those years ago. It is here he entrusted it to the two deities. Here it is safe. And here, as I write, I am safe. Nothing remains for me to do but take the goblet to the ruined abbey on the hill and place it with the bones of Bishop Cian and his sister. Then will the evil leave the O'Horgans. Now it can be written here in the safety of the sanctuary. As I wait for the full force of evil which comes at four a.m., as usual, on July the nineteenth each year, I know that my great-nephew, Cian, will inherit a house which will be reso—*'

She stopped and looked at me with surprise.

'Go on,' I said.

'That's all.' She looked at the back of the page. Blank. 'There's nothing more. That's it.'

'That's it?' I looked through the other sheets of paper to see if they'd got mixed up. It was then I noticed the date on the first page.

'July the nineteenth,' I said. A tight feeling

seemed to grip my head.

'What is it?' said Jo. 'Why have you gone white?'

'That's the date he died.' My voice came out like a strangled frog's. 'He was actually writing this when he died.'

CHAPTER TWELVE

'That's what Mrs Barry was trying to say to me,' I breathed.

'What?'

'She was saying "san". I couldn't make out what she was at. But that's it – sanctuary. She was trying to tell me about a sanctuary.'

'He was in the sanctuary when he died then,' said Jo. 'And he was feeling safe. He knew he couldn't be harmed as long as he was there. He could write his story without being harmed because this sanctuary is protected.'

'So, where is it?' I tried to keep the panic out of my voice. 'This sanctuary, where is it?'

Jo was shaking her head. 'Could be anywhere. At least we know it's somewhere in the house.'

'For heaven's sake!' I exploded. 'We have to find it! Four a.m.' I swallowed. 'The diary says that the full force of... of evil comes at four a.m.

He's not gone, Grimstone! He has a certain time... it's not over, Jo. It's only just starting! Jeez, I can't take any more.'

'For the last time, Cian!' she thumped my arm. 'We're this close. We have to see it through. I'm dead scared too, but I hate what that slimeball has done to our family. I hate him so much that I'm spitting angry. You can't desert now. *I'm* certainly not.'

I chewed my cheek. Of all the sisters going, why did I get a defiant Amazon with attitude?

'What time is it now?' she asked, not giving me time to back down. I turned fearfully to look at the kitchen clock which was ticking in the shadows.

'Nearly twenty-past three,' I gulped. 'We've a little over half an hour.'

'Mrs Barry!' put in Jo excitedly.

'What?'

'Mrs Barry will tell us where she found the old man. All we've to do is ring the hospital and get them to ask her.'

The simplicity of her solution left me gobsmacked. I almost hugged her.

'You're absolutely right. Phew! I thought we'd be searching—'

'Come on then,' Jo cut across my relief. 'No time to lose.'

We dashed over to the kitchen phone.

'The number,' said Jo. 'The hospital number...'

'I know it,' I replied. I remembered it from earlier. A good memory is one asset at least that I can boast of.

I took a deep breath before lifting the receiver. 'With our luck, I bet the darn lines are down,' I said.

'Well, would you ever pick it up and try?' snapped Jo. 'You're wasting time.'

I closed my eyes and exulted with a 'Yessss' when I heard the beautiful dial tone.

Jo gave a big sigh and squeezed my hand.

I shifted from one foot to the other as the ringing went on and on at the hospital number. I bit my lip. 'Come on, come on. There has to be somebody there. It's a hospital for heaven's sake!'

'It's a small hospital.' Jo tried to sound consoling, but she couldn't keep the rising panic out of her voice. 'They probably don't have someone at reception all night—' She broke off when a voice cut in.

'Glenderry Memorial Hospital. Can I help you?'

Skip the preliminaries, I thought. Get to the point, Cian.

'Listen,' I began. 'There was an old lady, called Mrs Barry, admitted earlier today. She sprained her ankle—'

'Are you a relative?'

'No. But there's something I must find out from her—'

'Excuse me?' The voice was beginning to sound a tad on the snooty side.

'I'm ringing from Glenderry House,' I went on. 'I'm... I'm the new owner. I need to ask Mrs Barry something important!'

'Is this some kind of joke, sonny?' The tone was really acid now. 'It's half-past three in the morning and you want to disturb a patient?'

'I know. Look, you don't understand. Weird things are happening here—'

'Weird things are happening here too,' snapped the voice. 'This is a hospital. You could be preventing an emergency call from getting through.'

'This *is* an emergency!' I screamed. 'It's not a joke. You've got to ask Mrs Barry—'

'I don't have to do anything, sonny, except tell you to go to blazes and get off this phone. Play your game elsewhere.'

'No, wait,' I tried to sound reasonable. 'My mother is there. She's staying with Mrs Barry. Her name is Mrs O'Horgan. Please ask her to come to the phone. We're being attacked, me and my sister. Please!'

'If you're being attacked, sweetheart, I don't know why you're ringing a hospital. Ring the police. Now, get off this phone.'

'Please—' I began. But the voice had been replaced by the dial tone.

'Oh, God!' breathed Jo.

'She didn't believe me,' I muttered helplessly.

'Ring the police,' said Jo.

'What?'

'She said to ring the police.'

I looked at her with scorn. 'What good do you think that'll do? Do you think they'll arrest Grimstone? Throw him in the slammer for being a spook? Besides, the river has burst its banks and we're completely cut off, or had you forgotten?'

Jo bit her lip. 'Ring them anyway,' she said. 'They might be able to tell us what to do.'

'Yeah,' I retorted. 'Like, there's a special

handbook for policemen, "How to Deal with Ghastly Ghouls and Screaming Spooks". Get real.'

'No, you clown,' retorted Jo. 'But at least we won't be going through all this on our own.'

Her voice was drowned by a roll of thunder. Of course she was right, I thought.

'You're a doll,' I told Jo. 'Why didn't I think of that? They might even know where the old man was found. There was probably an inquest – there usually is when someone is found dead.'

'Well, go on then,' urged Jo. 'Dial. We don't have much time.'

I picked up the receiver again. This time I wouldn't be so hysterical, I told myself. This time I would be calm and MAKE them believe me. I began to dial. As I pressed the second button, the soft glow of candlelight was replaced by a searing flash of lightning, followed by an earth-trembling rumble of thunder. The phone clicked and then... nothing. I pressed the receiver with panicky urgency, but the phone was quite dead.

'It's started,' whispered Jo. 'The whole thing has started.'

I stared at her with horrified disbelief, the fleas on rollerblades once more skating up my scalp.

Another flash of lightning prompted me into further frantic pressing on the receiver. Still no sound.

Jo's face was white and tense as she stood in frozen terror. She suddenly jerked back to reality and, grabbing a candle, she made a beeline for the cupboard beside the range.

'What are you at?' I shouted as she began rummaging with one hand, throwing things out.

'A torch,' she called back over another clap of thunder. 'There has to be a… ha!' She finished with a note of triumph and held up a good, strong torch. She shone the beam of light around the kitchen and gave a cry of satisfaction.

'At least we won't have to depend on flimsy candlelight,' she said.

I replaced the receiver, musing on the fact that my sister was one sharp kid. 'I was just going to suggest that,' I said. 'About looking for a torch.'

Jo was now gathering up the pages off the sofa. 'We have to find that sanctuary,' she looked up at me. 'What was it the old man had written?'

'That he found it under the Stars of Christianity and the Sword of Cian of the Tuatha de Danaan,' I replied. It's easy to remember something that has your name on it.

'Think hard,' went on Jo. 'The house was built around this sanctuary—'

'So it must be on the ground floor,' I finished. At least we wouldn't have to go prowling about upstairs.

'He says it was hidden for all those years,' Jo said, trying to find the page. 'So it must be behind a wall or something.'

'Start here, in the kitchen,' I suggested. It wasn't so much that I expected to find anything as that I was reluctant to leave its familiar warmth.

We set about tapping the walls and pulling open the big presses. Nothing.

'It's twenty to four,' Jo said, her voice shaking. 'I'm scared, Cian.' She clutched at my sweater.

Twenty minutes, I thought. Twenty minutes to finish what the old man had started. I glanced for one confused second at the back door. No, I couldn't do a runner now.

'Twenty minutes to kick this spook up the backside and send him crawling back to his corner for good,' I said.

Brave words. Inside my head my brains were freaking out.

CHAPTER THIRTEEN

'Nothing,' said Jo. 'No hidden walls here.'

'We're going to have to search all of the ground floor.' I shuddered at the thought.

'Oh cripes,' whispered Jo.

'We could still do a runner,' I offered, despite my snap decision only moments ago. Strange thing courage, it comes and goes like a broken telly – one minute the picture is clear, the next it's lost in fuzziness. 'All we've to do is open the back door and—'

Jo's skinny little body straightened up and she looked at me with glittering eyes.

'We will not,' she said with jaw-thrusting determination. 'I'm not going to have this... this rotten creep of a thing muscling in on our family for the rest of our days. Do I have to keep saying this to you? We'll sort it out. Come on.'

I followed her to the door. We hesitated for

just one second before I pulled it open. The sudden blast of cold air from the hall hit us like a wet dishcloth.

'Back to the dining room!' shouted Jo as another flash of lightning illuminated the kitchen behind us.

We dashed along the hall, me keeping my hand cupped over the candle I was still holding, Jo flashing the torch. The dining room still smelled of the candles we'd lit here earlier. It was a big, dreary place with a huge table and high-backed chairs that loomed like square-shouldered Inquisitors in the dim light.

'This place hasn't been used in years,' I said. 'Bet nobody ever had so much as a plate of chips here.'

'Start searching,' said Jo. 'You take that side, I'll take this.'

Once more we tapped and prodded.

'Nothing—' I began. I froze as a big clock on the mantelpiece chimed the quarter-hour.

Jo gave a whimper from across the room. Neither of us said the obvious – that we had fifteen minutes left before whatever it was that had terrorized my great-uncle and his ancestors would take on two petrified youngsters.

'Come on,' I said.

We passed frantically from the dining room to a drawing room where the furniture was draped with dust sheets. Any other time their spooky appearance would have given me the creeps, but right now we were up against the real thing. We pulled open the big cupboard doors beside the sideboard and tapped for a comforting hollow sound. Nothing. From there we went back to the study and drew another blank.

'There's no sign of any hidden room!' Jo's voice was almost hysterical. She was back clutching my sweater.

'There has to be.' I held her torch hand and shone the beam all around. 'If Mrs Barry found the old man there, then it HAS to be visible. She'd hardly conceal it again. Let's have a look at the writing again, see if there's anything we've missed.'

We sat on the bottom step of the stairs and Jo took the pages from under her sweater. She shone the light over the words until we came to the phrase, *the Stars of Christianity to guide and the Sword of Cian of the Tuatha de Danaan to protect* .

'We have to look for those signs,' I said. Now my voice was beginning to break – not in an adolescent way but in a shrill, terrified way.

The next rumble was not thunder; it was the hall door being thumped.

'It's back,' Jo whispered.

We sat, hypnotized with petrified fascination, waiting for the door to be thrown open. Which it was. The dim, blue light which hurtled down the hall was followed by a stifling heat far worse than anything we had experienced earlier. Both of us gagged at the cloying warmth that took our breath away. I threw my snuffed candle at whatever was screeching at us from the doorway. Snatching the torch from Jo, I tried shining it in the direction of the sound. At least if we saw a face we'd know what we were up against – there is nothing so frightening as the unknown. But the beam was simply swallowed up in a darkness that was greater than any light. Whatever was out there wasn't calling for cocoa and chat.

I grabbed Jo's arm and roughly pulled her up the stairs. We stumbled along the corridor and fell into the first room we met, shutting the door behind us. We leaned against it, panting. The rumbling from downstairs was making the floor shake under our feet. How long before Grimstone the Ghoul would seek us up here?

'We've done it now,' gasped Jo. 'What did you want to drag me up here for?'

'What do you mean?' I shone the light on her and she blinked.

'We'll never find that sanctuary now,' she replied, pushing the torch away. 'It certainly won't be upstairs if the house was built around it.'

I gritted my teeth. She was quite right. We were farther from finding the safe place than we could ever be.

'Damn!' I hissed. We fell into an uneasy silence while we listened to the sounds below us. 'We can't go down now,' I said after a while. 'We can't go down there while that's going on.'

'So, what do we do?' asked Jo.

I shrugged. Now I really wished I'd listened to myself and hit the road, flooded or not.

Jo grabbed my sleeve. 'Listen,' she whispered.

I didn't need to be told to listen; the heavy thumping was coming up the stairs. Every nerve in my body seemed to scream out at once. Jo was scrabbling at the lock.

'What are you doing?' I breathed.

'A key.' Her voice was shaking. 'There must be a key.'

'Don't bother, Jo.'

127

She looked up at me quizzically.

'There's no point. No keys or bolts will keep that thing out. He'll go where he wants to go.'

She put her hands to her face in a gesture of defeat. Then she pointed to a lumpy bed with a frilly thing around the bottom.

'At least let's hide,' she pleaded. 'We've got to do something.'

We dashed across the room and flung ourselves under the bed, trying not to cough in the cloud of dust we'd raised. I turned out the torch and we held tightly to one another. It was like waiting for a guillotine to fall on your neck or for a hangman to pull open the trap door that would leave you swinging. Except that this was ten times worse. At least if you were being executed you could nod to the executioner and wish him a lingering drowning in pig's vomit. But this was horror beyond any human understanding.

The thumping was in the corridor now. I could feel Jo burying her face in her arms. Maybe if I did that too, maybe if we both hid our faces, we wouldn't see him and he wouldn't see us. He'd just toddle back to try again another night. By then we'd be gone. Whatever Jo might say about resolving this curse, my courage was back on fuzzy reception again.

We both screamed when the door was flung open. The dim, blue light darted back and forth, finally stopping at the place where we were hiding. The heavy, dark presence entered the room, filling it with the now-familiar stench and sticky warmth. The floor shook as the sound came towards us. We scrambled out on the far side of the bed. There was an inhuman roar and we were attacked with a wind so ferocious that it knocked us down.

Just as suddenly as it started, it stopped – at least around me. The roaring continued, but all I could feel was the clammy presence. I switched on the torch and shone it in the direction of Jo's screams. What I saw made me gasp; the skinny kid was being buffeted by such force her feet were off the ground.

'Hey!' I yelled, running towards her. 'Leave her alone!'

She plummeted to the floor, only to be whipped up again. I was dumbfounded. I was the one who was supposed to be at the receiving end of this creep's venom. With courage born of momentary insanity, I stood up and shone the light on myself.

'I'm Cian!' I shouted. 'You big jerk, it's me you want.'

But Jo continued to be tossed about, screaming.

I was desperate. What did he want with my little sister? And then the picture focused for me. I realized Jo was still clutching the old man's manuscript. I tried to remember his words. Nobody had ever succeeded in writing down the history of events because this spook had always prevented it.

'That's it!' I cried. 'Jo, give me the manuscript!'

She hit the wall with a thud as unseen hands tore at her. With a superhuman effort I reached her and wrenched the papers from her grasp. The forced turned on me.

'I have it,' I yelled over the howling fury. 'I have the written word. It tells where the goblet is!' Then I tore the pages in two and tossed them into the blackness. I grabbed Jo and ran for the door.

That might keep him occupied for a second or two, I thought. 'We've got to get downstairs – got to get away from here. There's nothing we can do. We're out of here.'

Jo didn't protest. Even if she had, I had every intention of making a speedy exit.

We'd reached the bottom step before the house again reverberated with the violence from above. With a start I realized the front door was blocked by the blue light, its shifting shape filled with menace. We backed away.

'The back door!' I panted, pulling at Jo again. Please don't let the back door be blocked too. Would we ever get out into the welcome normality of feeling the rain on our faces?

Halfway down the hall Jo pulled me to a stop.

'Jo!' I cried. 'We can't stop now. Hold on to me and—'

She was trying to catch her breath as she pulled me towards a door under the stairs.

'I remember,' she wheezed. 'Mum sent me to get a sweeping brush. I tried here—'

'For crying out loud, Jo!' I shouted. 'Have you gone doolally? A sweeping brush wouldn't be any use against—'

She shook her head impatiently and pulled open the small door. 'I remember I got a funny smell, an earthy smell. Come on, it's our only chance.'

The kid's gone cracked, I thought. That spook has made her raving mad. Short of dumping her here in the middle of this ghastly circus, I'd no choice but to follow. I shone the torch around the small cubbyhole and felt my innards drop in despair.

'Ho!' I wailed. 'There's nothing here, only Hoovers and stuff. You've dragged us straight into a trap. Now we're rightly up the creek!'

As if on cue, the fearful thuds of approaching evil stopped outside the door we'd just come through. We pressed our hands to our ears, almost losing the precious torch, as an almighty howl, which seemed to come from the depths of the earth, filled the small closet.

'Look!' Jo shouted.

I was so confused now that I couldn't focus on anything. Jo grabbed the torch from me and shone it over a shelf with old paint tins on it.

'The signs!' she went on. 'Look, Cian—'

What happened next will always remain as a jumble in my mind. No matter how I try to recall it, the scene is always a blur. An evil presence, smelling of death and decay, took over the whole closet with smothering power. I knew I was being pulled towards it, but my limbs were not responding to my commands to fight it. I was shouting a lot, I know that. I vaguely remember Jo, with the torch in one hand, opening a door under the shelf with the paint tins on it. I remember thinking, with the most stupid lack of logic, that she'd ruin her clothes and Mum would be furious. My body had gone totally limp, had gone totally beyond the horror in here with us. There was no fight left, just submission to this power that was taking me over, lulling me into its clutches. And the heat. I still get the urge to throw up when I remember the sweaty heat that made me gasp for breath.

But my strongest memory is of Jo, standing at this doorway, watching me being pulled away. Only it wasn't Jo – at least it was and it wasn't. How can you describe a face that keeps changing? One moment it was skinny little Jo, the next it was someone who looked very like Jo except that she had a long dress and a plait of fair hair. The faces kept merging, one into the other, like an overlay you get in one of those science books that shows you how the brain works.

My particular brain was not working very well just then. This howling fury continued to wrap itself round me and I was letting it do so. That is until a broom handle hit me squarely across the shoulders and made me yelp into action. The Jo/lady-with-plait figure was pulling me towards the door. It was when she pushed herself in front of me I realized that the lady was the bishop's sister. It was like *déjà vu*, following exactly the same confrontation I'd seen in the virtual reality dream I'd had earlier.

'Go,' she said, in a voice that wasn't Jo's. 'Take your evil to damnation with you.' She was looking squarely at the turbulent black mass that was still dragging and pulling at me.

Then I remembered the sequence of events in that dream. What had happened then was about to happen again – Grimstone had killed the sister who stood before the bishop, just as her figure, now merged with Jo's, was standing in front of me now.

'Jo!' I shrieked. I grabbed her just as a swirling, shapeless mass of black descended on her. With a scream she fell back on top of me as I pulled her through the small doorway. We lay waiting for the cloying evil to overcome us, but nothing followed us through the door. I kicked the door shut.

'Jo? Jo! Are you all right?' I cried. The torch,

still shining, was thrown in a corner, casting eerie shadows in this place. 'Where are we?' I reached for the torch and shone it around. We were in a small, round chamber made of stones. A shabby easy chair covered with a blanket stood against one wall. On a small card table beside it was an old portable typewriter. Sheets of blank paper lay scattered around. This was it, this was the place where my great-uncle had found refuge from the thing that had turned him into a lonely recluse. And to think that he'd died here, just when he was at the point of banishing all of that. It didn't seem fair.

'A beehive hut,' I breathed.

'What?' A very dazed Jo was struggling to her feet.

'We're in the ruins of a beehive hut – the sort of place monks slept in. The house was built around a beehive hut which was kept hidden all those years!'

'You're sure?' Jo said, rubbing her head.

'We're here!' I said excitedly. 'We're in the sanctuary, Jo. Your hunch was right.' And then I did something really weird; I hugged her until she gasped for breath.

'This is the place,' I went on. 'This is where

the old man was the night he wrote the story. Remember? He said nothing could harm him here. We're safe, Jo.'

'That's it.' Jo's head was clearing now. 'Mum sent me for a sweeping brush because she'd knocked over a tray of Waterford glass and didn't want Mrs Barry to find out – so she sent me to see if there was one under the stairs. I remember the smell. Like the time Dad took us to that ancient burial place in Newgrange, there was the same earthy smell. It came to me when we were running from that blue light. It suddenly dawned on me that it was more than just a closet.' She stopped and looked at me in the dim light. 'But listen.'

We both stood still. The noise from outside was louder than before. The circular stone wall that surrounded us shook, sending bits of rubble and dust raining on our heads.

'I don't think he'll follow,' Jo said, as if to convince herself. 'The signs, they're over the door outside. The Sword of Cian of the whatsits and the Stars of Christianity – they're there, in very faint colour over the door.'

'Then we're protected,' I put in. 'It's OK, he can howl until his poxy throat cracks, but we're safe here.'

Another shower of rubble blunted my words somewhat.

'Then the goblet must be here,' said Jo. 'The old man said it was hidden here, remember?'

Trying to keep the howling in its proper perspective, we kept telling ourselves that it couldn't harm us as we set about looking for the goblet.

It didn't take us long. I found the small slab in a niche under what appeared to be a stone seat.

'Is that it?' I asked, lifting out what looked like a tin mug with two handles. 'Is this what all the fuss was about? This little bit of a thing? I was expecting something like the Ardagh Chalice. This is so small it fits in one hand – look. It just couldn't be what gremlin Grimstone out there is after. This is like something Mum would pick up at a car-boot sale.'

'Show me, give it here,' said Jo. She spat on the cuff of her sweater and rubbed a small part of the goblet. Several spits and rubs later, we both took a sharp breath. A dullish yellow shine was beginning to show through the grime.

'Gold,' whispered Jo. 'Celtic gold! This is a beautiful little thing.' She spat again and de-grimed a few more areas. Now we could make out a silver band with faces hammered onto it which surrounded the base. The two handles were made from fantastic creatures which were biting their own tails. A cross, set with stones of some sort, was incised on one side. A Celtic whirly design decorated the other side.

'Dual Deity,' I whispered.

'What?' said Jo. The howling outside was reaching another crescendo.

'Dual Deity – Christian and Celtic,' I shouted.

'What do we do now?' asked Jo.

'Good point,' I replied. 'Wait, I suppose.'

'Wait for what? Until him out there brings this place crashing around our ears? Are you sure we're safe?'

I had to admit it wasn't looking that way as another load of rubble cascaded down, shifting some of the stones.

'He's not going to give in, is he?' Jo continued, her shoulders drooping from exhaustion and despair.

CHAPTER FOURTEEN

The atmosphere in the small chamber became stifling. Jo took off her sweater and wiped the perspiration from her forehead with it. Even in the dim light I could see the bruises on her shoulders from the buffeting she'd had upstairs. I was overcome with a mixture of guilt and pity for this tough little lady who was here in this mess on my behalf.

'You're OK, kid,' I said.

'I'm what?' She stopped mopping her brow and looked at me.

'You're a great kid. I'm glad you're my sister.'

'Will you knock it off,' she scoffed. 'Your brain's gone soft. More to the point, what do we do now?'

I had at least expected gratitude, but I should have known better.

'I don't know what to do,' I snapped. 'Would I

be sitting here if I knew what to do?'

The rumbling outside continued, the dust and rubble still dislodging onto our heads. Jo now put the sweater over her head. The heat was overpowering. Even though Grimstone's wraith was outside, the heat and stench pervaded every part of the hut.

'We'll roast to death,' said Jo.

The sweat was running into my eyes. I wiped them with my sleeve, but even my sleeve felt hot.

'If I wipe my eyes any more they'll turn to mush,' I groaned.

Jo gave a short scream as one of the stones that made up the beehive hut crashed at our feet.

'We're trapped!' she shrieked, thrashing about with her arms. 'We're trapped here. He's going to bury us alive!'

'Hold on,' I shouted over the noise. 'Calm down, Jo!' I tried grabbing her arms, but panic had given her extra strength and I simply succeeded in getting a belt on the nose. Now it was my turn to panic as another rock tumbled out of the wall.

'You rotten ghoul!' I shouted, flailing at the rough wall with my fists. 'You stupid… stupid…' I sank, sobbing to the earthen floor.

Jo threw herself down beside me, wrapping the goblet in her sweater. 'Cian,' she whimpered, her dirty face tracked with sweat and tears. 'Are we going to die?'

I wished I could say something more than 'Mmmppff,' but I was melting into a quivering blob.

'He died here,' Jo shrieked. 'Great-uncle Cian died here! It's going to kill us too, don't you see? We're not safe!'

'He was old,' I tried to reason. 'He had a heart attack—'

'We'll have heart attacks too,' went on Jo. 'Or smother. I'm going to smother, Cian. I can't breathe. Maybe we should give him the goblet. Maybe we should just throw it out the door and… and…'

It was tempting, but a sudden rush of blood to my scrambled brain recalled my promise to Bishop Cian. He had looked directly at me and I had made a promise. This time it was my turn to push out the courage weapon.

'I promised,' I said to Jo. 'I promised Bishop Cian.'

She frowned and flung herself down beside me again. 'Brave words,' she said. 'But how will you carry out the promise? God, I'm so confused! I didn't think it would end like this.'

I sank even further onto the ground – my mind clinging to noble thoughts, my body trying to bury itself like a demented mole.

We sat side by side, listening to the howls which never ceased. What was the creep up to? Was he trying to bring the sanctuary down around our heads and then come for the goblet from another angle, thus avoiding crossing the lintel with the protection signs on it? That seemed about right. Better not say this to Jo, I thought.

Nothing seemed to matter now, all fight was drained from both of us. The stinking, sweaty heat filled every pore. When another pile of dusty rubble dumped on my head and ran with the perspiration down my neck, I hadn't the energy to wipe it away. I shut my eyes and hoped death would get to me before the thing outside did.

What was shaking me? Death doesn't shake you before he hauls you off, does he?

'Ouch!' Death doesn't pinch either.

'How can you sleep at a time like this, you big eejit?' Jo's filthy face peered at me. 'Wake up and look!'

'What?' I tried to gather my poached brains and body together.

'There.' Jo was pointing across the hut.

'I can't see anything,' I began.

'Will you look!' hissed Jo. 'That big stone.'

'Good grief!' I exclaimed. 'Daylight.'

The big stone which Jo was pointing out was slightly dislodged, revealing the first light of dawn. We were that close to the outside world. Putting all thoughts of death on rewind, I scrambled across the hut.

'Come on, help me,' I said.

The two of us heaved and pushed, our sweaty hands slipping on the smooth surface of the rock. At first it didn't budge, but, with a surge of renewed strength, I wasn't about to give up. If I had to die, I'd prefer to burst my heart trying to escape than lie in wait for some geek with an odour problem.

'It's moving,' panted Jo.

Sure enough the welcome sound of rock grinding on rock told us that our efforts were paying off. After a few more heaves I shouted to Jo to stand back. As she stood behind me, I gave the rock one final push and it crashed to the ground.

'Air,' I gasped. 'Fresh air. I'll never take it for granted again.'

We stood for a brief moment, filling our lungs and savouring the cool, damp atmosphere. However, there was no time to be lost. As Jo held on to the goblet, still wrapped in her sweater, I hoisted her up to the opening left by the rock.

'The church!' she exclaimed from the ledge. 'The church is straight ahead, up the hill.'

That made sense. A monk's living quarters would be near to the place of worship. Those boys liked to be close to the action.

'Let's get the goblet to those tombs,' I called up to her.

I clambered up after her and we both hopped down into the long, wet grass below. The small hole we'd come through was surrounded by crumbling bricks and plaster. It was easy to see how, over the centuries, it had become built over and obliterated. The present house, as Mrs Barry had said, was built in the seventeen hundreds, but it had been built on the site of other houses, going back, possibly, to Bishop Cian's nephew. If the silly prat had only looked through the ruined beehive hut before he built his house over it, he'd have saved a lot of big-eared people a lot of pain.

Then again, he probably thought he was insuring his home against evil by absorbing a holy man's cell into it. Pathetic, really. One should at least look at the signs over a door before plastering over. Great-uncle Cian must have felt so excited when he uncovered the doorway and the signs. All those years of searching...

'Come on,' shouted Jo impatiently. Although it was still raining and the clouds overhead were leaden and grey, it was still comforting to see that it was dawn, however dull. I glanced back fearfully, expecting to see a massive shape pursue us, but there was nothing. Daylight, I thought, remembering all the vampire films I'd seen. That lot don't hang about in daylight, any film director worth his salt knows that. I took another breath of that great air and ran after Jo.

'Hurry,' she called.

'It's OK,' I said, voice, bones and brain returning to normal. 'It's daybreak. We're safe now.'

We both giggled with the hysterical laughter that released all the pent-up tension of the awful night. The rain on our faces washed away some of the grime as we ran up the hill.

'Just think,' said Jo, holding her sweater with

the precious goblet aloft. 'In a few minutes we'll have saved this family from that hellish spook. You and me – two kids. We did it, Cian!'

'We sure did,' I laughed, twirling around in a jubilant dance. Below us we could see the river, its banks burst to fill several fields with a torrential force that swept bushes and gateposts along with it. The road had completely disappeared.

'Will you look at that!' I said to Jo. 'We really were cut off. There's no way we'd have got across.'

'Will you come on, for heaven's sake,' shouted Jo. 'You're wasting time.'

The ruined church loomed through the curtain of rain, its wall overhung with ivy. Small slabs of sandstone stood in higgledy-piggledy fashion around the outside.

'Monks' graves,' said Jo.

'How do you know that?' I asked. 'Don't tell me, I know. You read Dad's crummy books.'

'No, smartass,' she retorted. 'My pal, Lucy, has a CD-ROM about stuff like that. Anyway,' she put a hand on her hip, 'are you sure that the bishop and his sister are buried inside? That they're not under some of these?'

'Nope, definitely not. Both tombs are inside. All we have to do is—'

Jo had skipped ahead and was almost at the arched doorway.

She turned and grinned at me through the rain. Her skinny little figure seemed distorted and out of shape.

'Move your big smelly feet,' she teased. 'Cian! Cian? What are you stopping for? Come on, stop messing. That's not funny any more.'

I tried to shout to her, tried to tell her about the blue light that was glimmering behind her, but I couldn't move.

'I'll kill you, Cian. I really will. Get up here—'

It was then that she saw the light herself. Her scream jerked me into action. Jo had the goblet – she was in danger! I sprinted the last few yards and reached her just as the now-too-familiar howl came from within the ruin.

'It's in there!' gasped Jo. 'It's in the church.'

My first impulse was to run, but something kept me there. To this day I don't know whether it was the immobility of cowardice or else some strong force from past ancestors that kept me there. I prefer to think it was the latter. Through the gloom inside the ruin, I could just make out the ominous shadow that drifted around the altar area. All my fear was spent. I simply hadn't the energy for any more fear.

'Bog off,' I whispered, tears of frustration stinging my eyes. 'Just bog off.'

The warm, cloying atmosphere drew me inside. This time, I knew, there would be no escape. I grabbed Jo's arm before I went through the arch and took the sweater from her. I clutched it to my chest.

'Get away!' I whispered, barely loud enough for her to hear above the rumbling within. 'Don't stop until you come to the river. Grab a branch or something—'

'Cian, no!' she cried.

Every part of me shouted out to run too, but mentally I was beyond flight.

'Do it!' I shouted, never taking my eyes off the shapeless menace that now drifted in my direction.

'I'm here, you creep,' I muttered. 'I'm Cian O'Horgan.'

I had figured that it would claim me, the last Cian O'Horgan, with a swift, wasting blow. I wasn't prepared for the violent preamble to death, a toying like a cat with a mouse. I was thrown against the rough stone wall, all my breath forced out of my body. Self-preservation returned with the second blow and I began to fight back. But how can you fight something you can't even feel?

The warm stench invaded my nose as if it would take over my whole body. I needed to throw up, but I couldn't. I vaguely recognized Jo's shouting as I was being tossed about. She should know, I thought. She'd been through this. But, deep inside, I knew that this spook wanted *me*. I was to pay the full price – my life and the goblet. I could have done with my bishop ancestor, headless or otherwise, to give a bit of assistance. But something told me it was up to me now. I was on my own. I groaned as the warm, deathly stench enveloped me and I braced myself for another slap into the wall. The physical fear of being hurt was nothing compared to the terror of this faceless being. With each blow, the stench and the suffocating warmth got stronger and stronger until I could take no more. I lifted the bundle over my head.

'There!' I cried. I threw it towards a clump of grass and fell to the ground, sobbing. I had given the thing what it wanted. I had let down the people who, for years, had protected this precious little goblet. All that ordeal last night had now come to nothing. I had failed myself and everybody who'd gone before me.

As if through a haze, I saw Jo dash across the aisle and throw herself on a slab.

'Jo!' I tried to cry out, but all that came out was a strangled yelp. Just before I passed out.

When I came to, Jo was wiping my face with wet leaves.

'About time,' she grunted, but I could see that she was relieved. I struggled up and looked around.

Not a spook in sight. Not so much as a smell or a hint of warmed-up death.

'What the hell happened?' I asked, considering which bruise to nurse first.

Jo was grinning. How could she do a stupid thing like grin when I had just sold the family up the proverbial river?

'I put the goblet into that hole,' she said, pointing to the slab I'd been lying on.

'You what? Jo, didn't you see?' I whined. 'I threw the goblet at that blasted spook. I gave it to him, Jo. Don't you understand?'

She was shaking her head. 'You threw my sweater at him,' she said calmly. 'I had the goblet.'

'You couldn't—'

She looked up at me and grinned again.

'In my knickers,' she said. 'I had it tucked into my knickers. I figured something like this just might happen. While you were doing your daft dance on the hill, I shoved the goblet into my knickers.'

CHAPTER FIFTEEN

'She's fine,' Mum said as I held back at the hospital door. 'You watch too many hospital dramas. It was only a slight scare, she'll be out in a day or two. Now, come on.'

Mum had to reassure me that there would be no tubes or wires shoved up Mrs Barry's nose and no telly screens bleeping. That would have freaked me out.

Mrs Barry was sitting up in bed. She was wearing a fuzzy orange bed jacket that made her look like an elderly teddy bear. She put down the magazine and beamed at us.

'What beautiful flowers,' she said, pushing herself up to a better position.

Jo grinned as she put the big bunch on the locker beside the bed. Mrs Barry leaned over and smelled them. 'Phlox,' she said, breathing deeply. 'And woodbine and poppies. Is there anything as nice as wild flowers?'

'We got them up at the old ruined church,' said Jo.

Mrs Barry froze. A perplexed look crossed her plump face.

'No,' she whispered. 'Nothing grows there.'

Mum laughed. 'Well, this must be a good year,' she said. 'The place is covered with flowers. Must be after all that rain. The children brought me up there this afternoon. It's a beautiful spot. We're going to have a picnic there when you come home. You never told me that there was such a wonderful view behind the house. With the sun shining and the birds singing and all these wonderful flowers – you've been keeping all that a secret, Mrs Barry.' She laughed again and wagged her finger at the dumbstruck old lady.

Mrs Barry sank back on her pillows. 'Birds? Sunshine?' she shook her head.

'It's true,' put in Jo. 'It looks super.'

Mrs Barry looked at me. I smiled and nodded. But I saw that she just couldn't take all this on board.

'Yeah, that's right,' I said. 'It's fine. Everything is... everything is in its right place.'

Realization suddenly dawned.

'You mean…?' she began.

'There, you see,' said Mum. 'Even an old grump like Cian thinks it's a nice spot.' She looked up and down the ward. 'Never a nurse around when you want one. Never mind, I'll take these flowers out and find something to put them into. They'll droop in that evening sun if we don't get them into water.'

Mrs Barry waited until Mum had left the ward. Then she put her freckled hand on my arm.

'What's all this about flowers and sunshine? I told you, lad, that nothing much grows up on that hill. The sun never reaches it. And there's always a shadow around the ruined church. Ask anybody.'

'Not any more,' broke in Jo. 'You'll see.'

'I put the goblet back,' I said with just the right touch of drama. No point in going through an ordeal like last night if you can't amaze someone – especially since she was the only person who *could* be told.

The kick on my shin made me yelp.

'Excuse me,' growled Jo. 'Run that by us again, mister.'

I gave her a sickly grin and turned to Mrs Barry. 'It was Jo who actually dropped it into a break on the slab,' I set the record straight. 'Between us we outsmarted old Smellyspook.'

And so we told her the whole story. Now and then she interrupted with a 'God help us!' or 'Is that a fact?'

'It was the bishop's sister who got us through to the sanctuary,' said Jo. 'It was like… like she was part of me.' She paused, then went on, 'It was her I was thinking of most of the time. All during the most awful bits, I was thinking of her.'

'What do you mean?' I asked. 'Was she inside your head?'

'Don't be daft. No, ever since you told me the story,' went on Jo, 'I kept thinking of that brave sister. She died trying to protect her brother and, all through the years, nobody seems to have ever mentioned her name. It was bishop's sister this and bishop's sister that. Just because she was a woman she hardly got a mention. Makes you sick, doesn't it?'

Mrs Barry smiled. 'You're some woman yourself, Jo.'

I glanced at my sister, expecting her to blush at the compliment and go all coy. Not Jo. She leaned her elbows on the bed and nodded her head. 'Yeah, I am,' she said.

'Well, we know her name now,' I said lamely.

'That's right,' said Jo. 'Do you know what her name was, Mrs Barry?'

Mrs Barry shook her head.

'Johanna!' Jo exulted. 'Imagine that! When we cleared all the ivy and stuff off her tomb, we were able to read her name. Johanna – almost the same name as me.'

'No wonder she was keeping an eye on you. It's as if you and Cian were herself and her brother over again…'

'With the same names,' put in Jo.

'How did you find great-uncle Cian?' I asked Mrs Barry.

She shook her head at the memory. 'There was no sign of him when I came up that morning,' she said. 'I knew he couldn't be gone far. I was concerned because it was that time of year. You know?' She looked at me. I nodded. 'Then I saw the door under the stairs was open. When I went in I saw that everything had been pulled about, as if a bomb had hit it. I remember being shocked. I thought someone had broken in because, every other year there would always be a mess, but nothing as bad as this. I started clearing away some of the chaos, and then I saw the doorway under the shelves. I hadn't noticed that before. So I pushed it open and… and…' She looked at her hands and shook her head again.

'Why didn't you tell me?' I asked gently. 'If I'd known from the beginning about that sanctuary it would have saved us all that horror.'

'I know, lad. Believe me, I've lain here with my nerves in bits. But they had me doped with drugs. I couldn't speak. I kept wandering in and out of heavy sleep. I wanted to warn your mother, but every time I tried to speak, like the kind lady she is, she'd hush me up and tell me to relax. But, you see, I had thought I'd be with you. I thought I'd be there to guide you to it when the time was right.'

'It doesn't matter now,' put in Jo. 'After what we went through, we'll never be scared of anything again, will we, Cian?'

'Maybe,' I muttered. 'What about the Rock?' I said to Mrs Barry. 'I wonder what became of the Rock of Mohammed?'

She shrugged her fuzzy shoulders. 'Who knows? I expect it's safely hidden somewhere in Grimstone's land. And hopefully it will remain there – in peace.'

'Like the goblet is now,' added Jo.

'Just like the goblet,' agreed Mrs Barry. She smiled as she looked from Jo to me. 'I still can't believe it all,' she said.

'Can't believe what?' Mum bustled back into the ward, holding the flowers aloft in a glass vase. 'What don't you believe?'

'Ah,' Mrs Barry's cheeks wobbled and turned crimson. 'The, eh, weather. I can't believe how the weather has changed. It's the most wonderful change you could imagine. It's just too wonderful for words.'

I knew by Mum's face that she thought Mrs Barry was talking garbage.

'It's just a bit of sunshine, Mrs B,' she said.

Mrs Barry stretched out her arms and took a deep breath. 'Oh, beautiful sunshine,' she sighed.

'Must be something they've put her on,' Mum whispered to me. She fussed at the pillows behind Mrs Barry. 'You just rest there and get well,' she said loudly. 'Be ready for that picnic.'

'I'll look forward to that,' smiled Mrs Barry. 'You wouldn't believe how much I'll look forward to that.'

I turned at the door and gave her a wave. She gave me a thumbs-up sign and turned to smell the flowers.

'I was thinking,' I said to Mum as we drove from the hospital.

'That must have hurt,' put in Jo.

'I was thinking about the house,' I went on with dignity.

'Do you still want to sell it?' asked Mum.

'No!' I exclaimed. 'That's part of the family. I wouldn't sell it. What do you think I am? No, I was thinking that maybe Mrs Barry could run it as a guesthouse. She could go and live there and look after tourists. Until I'm old enough to take it on. What do you think?'

Mum turned to look at me, narrowly missing a passing fire engine on its way back from pumping the burst river banks.

'Is this the same lad who wanted nothing to do with "the mouldy old dump" only two days ago? What brought this on?'

Jo leaned forward and tugged my ears.

'The family ears brought it on,' she laughed. 'Ancestral ears.'

'Give over,' I muttered.

Mum had no idea what had gone on last night. By the time she'd arrived back at around noon, we had cleaned up ourselves and the house. Jo and I had talked about whether we should tell her or not.

'She'll never believe it,' I'd said. 'Besides, I haven't the energy to try and explain all this. It would be like… going through the whole thing again.'

Jo had nodded. 'Let's just leave it,' she'd said. 'It's over and done with. Maybe sometime when all this is well in the past…'

I yawned loudly and stretched my still-aching arms and legs. Jo lay along the back seat and planted her feet against the window.

'You two still tired?' asked Mum. 'I suppose you were up until all hours last night.'

'Pretty late,' I agreed. 'We were chasing spooks.'

'Of course you were,' laughed Mum.